As a Native American, Stanley Redfeather has always believed there was more to the world than what the average person could see. Learning about gargoyles and other paranormals is almost anti-climactic. Doing his job working as the foreman of his boss's massive cattle ranch continues as normal. Occasionally, having a bunch of gargoyles, vampires, and shifters around causes a little hiccup, especially when one of them finds their Fated mate, but for the most part, it's business as usual.

That changes when a trio of gargoyles arrive for a meeting, and after one sniff, one of them—Kultrak—claims Stanley is his Fated mate. Stanley knows what that means. He's supposed to be the other half of the gargoyle's soul, bond with him, and build a centuries-long life with him. While Stanley wouldn't mind having someone to share his solitary life with, he needs to know the gargoyle more than a day before trusting the male that they're perfect for each other.

When Stanley gets injured, will Kultrak's protectiveness in the face of the upcoming danger drive him away or draw him nearer?

Romancing the Foreman
Copyright © 2023 Charlie Richards
ISBN: 978-1-4874-3976-7
Cover art by Angela Waters

Published by eXtasy Books Inc

Look for us online at:
www.eXtasybooks.com

Romancing the Foreman
A Paranormal's Love 40

By

Charlie Richards

DEDICATION

If you're not moving forward, you're falling back.
~Sam Waterston

CHAPTER ONE

Stanley Redfeather stepped into the dining room, more than ready for the evening meal. After a day of wrestling cows for branding, he was filthy, tired, and starving. Plus, they were only half done.

I get to look forward to this for at least another day.

Still, Stanley wouldn't trade his job for anything. He'd served as ranch foreman to his boss, Nicholas Lindson, for the last decade. He'd taken over from his own father—Richard Redfeather—when he was thirty-two. At forty-two, he was no spring chicken, but he loved the outdoors, the animals, and the physicality of it.

Keeps me young.

"Hey, boss-man," Virgil greeted with a wide grin. The tawny-haired wrangler looked him up and down while chuckling softly. "Lookin' a little stiff, sir. Need me to ask Maggie for some muscle-relieving salve?"

"Laugh it up, Virgil," Stanley grumbled with a mock frown. "If you weren't a shifter, you'd be just as sore as me."

As a Native American, Stanley had always believed that there was more out there than what many humans thought. When Nicholas had brought home Bodb, revealing that gargoyles were real, Stanley hadn't been too shocked. The fact that Virgil, someone he'd worked with for several years, was a cougar shifter had been a bigger surprise. Stanley had wondered how he'd missed that.

Of course, then Stanley had realized that was the nature of paranormals. They hid in plain sight, carefully hiding their differences. Anonymity was their greatest defense against discrimination.

As sad as the fact was, every minority group in existence had been persecuted at one time or another. Some were still persecuted. Minority groups changed over the years, but the heart of man didn't seem to.

"Maybe not muscle sore, but that damn calf got me good, and I still feel it." Virgil's words drew Stanley out of his errant thoughts. The shifter was rubbing his thigh and shaking his head, his expression rueful. "Didn't move quite fast enough. I've already bruised."

Stanley recalled the young bull-calf that had managed to kick Virgil. He winced in sympathy.

"Bet Shaw was happy to massage some cream on it, though," Stanley teased, removing his moccasins and leaving them in the mudroom.

Virgil had recently found his fated mate in a small wombat shifter. According to their beliefs, the pair were bound at the soul level. They would never stray and were completely devoted to each other.

Stanley could admit, at least to himself, that the notion was sweet. Although, he couldn't imagine jumping in with both feet as fast as paranormals did once they found that special someone. Having been burned in a relationship more than once, Stanley didn't trust easily anymore.

One-offs every few months are just fine with me.

"Yep. Shaw helped me out plenty," Virgil agreed with an eyebrow waggle. With a shake of his head, he added, "After reading me the riot act for getting hurt, of course."

Stanley nodded as they both headed into the main house's huge dining room. He noticed Virgil had already showered, something he was still looking forward to doing. Stanley intended to eat fast and get back to his foreman's cottage to enjoy a soak in his jetted tub.

Perks of being the foreman.

The smell of the stew caused Stanley's stomach to rumble, and he hurried to the sideboard. A massive vat of the stuff already waited there. Grabbing a plate and a bread bowl, he did his best to ignore Virgil greeting Shaw with a deep kiss.

The wombat shifter helped Pauline—a fox shifter—in the kitchen. He also gave Mitchel a hand in his greenhouse, which was a new addition to the ranch. Pauline and Mitchel were mated with gargoyles—Lebone and Sindrid, respectively—and had joined them a few years back after Bodb had moved in. As it turned out, Bodb was a gargoyle elder—one of the ruling members of their race—and he always had at least two gargoyles patrolling the ranch for safety.

After filling his bread bowl with the hearty-looking beef stew, Stanley grabbed a beer from the mini-fridge under the sideboard and moved to the table. He placed his food and drink on it before settling in a chair. Stanley barely managed to keep in his sigh of pleasure at getting off his feet.

The first bite of his meal drew a contented grunt from Stanley. He'd never been more grateful than when Pauline and Lebone had arrived. She'd immediately taken over the kitchen, making it her own. While the housekeeper who'd retired just prior to Pauline's arrival had kept them fed, Pauline was so much better. Plus, being a fox shifter herself, no one needed to explain about making extra-huge meals for all the paranormals around.

Over the last couple of years, they'd even had a couple of vampires join them, which came in handy if a visiting client saw something they shouldn't. A vampire had the ability to peer into a human's mind and alter memories. That was how the species hid the fact that they were drinking a person's blood.

Stanley finished half his stew before tearing off a chunk of the bread bowl. After dipping it into the broth, he popped it into his mouth. He hummed appreciatively as he chewed.

Watching those around him tuck into their own meals, Stanley listened to the other men's sighs of pleasure and contentment. He smiled at his food, chewing another bite. For the most part, the only conversation was if someone wanted the salt or pepper passed.

Men and their food.

Finishing up his meal, Stanley contemplated getting seconds. He supposed he didn't really need it, but it sure tasted fantastic. Giving in, he rose and returned to the sideboard.

Besides, I still have over half my bread bowl. I'll just get a little.

Stanley peered over his shoulder at the over a dozen men — many in gargoyle form — and called, "Anyone want anything while I'm up?"

"Can I get some orange juice, please?" Maggie asked, smiling at him.

"Sure thing, sweet lady," Stanley replied.

"I could have gotten it, baby," Sandra claimed, her blonde brows creasing. The woman was very attentive to her lover, especially since Maggie carried their baby and was due any day now.

Maggie patted Sandra's hand. "I know, love." The darker-haired woman rolled a shoulder, saying, "But he was already up and offered."

Sandra didn't look convinced, but she nodded anyway.

"Here ya go, Maggie." Stanley placed the bottle of juice on the table beside her. Recalling Virgil's teasing comment, he decided it was actually a good one. "Do you happen to have any pain-relaxing ointment for muscles made up?"

Maggie happened to be a witch, and she made tonics, creams, and tinctures for them. Most medicines designed and used by humans didn't work on paranormals due to their higher metabolism. The stuff would burn through their system too fast to be effective.

Utilizing a small section of the greenhouse, Maggie grew a variety of medicinal plants and herbs. She used them to create her extracts. Maggie even made a potion for Ssimeas, a mated gargoyle.

Ssimeas was mated with a human named Attain. Under most circumstances, a gargoyle would eat cinnamon in order to render himself sterile, since gargoyles could impregnate their male fated mates. Ssimeas was a rare case where he was immune to the effects of cinnamon, and Attain was allergic, so he couldn't eat it either. Instead, Maggie's potion did the job.

"Absolutely," Maggie replied, picking up the orange juice. "I always make sure I have a couple of jars on hand, just in case." With a laugh, she stated, "Ranch life is hard work."

"That it is," Stanley agreed. Grinning, he told her honestly, "But I wouldn't trade it for anything."

"It is wonderful here," Maggie agreed. Turning to Sandra, she asked, "Can you run to my workshop and grab one of the small, green-labeled tubs?"

"Sure thing." Sandra bounced to her feet, obviously eager to please her lover.

"It can wait until you're done eating," Stanley told her, lifting a hand to stay her actions.

Sandra ignored him. "It's fine. Be right back."

Then Sandra hustled from the room.

Maggie chuckled and shrugged, giving Stanley a *what can you do* look before refocusing on her meal.

Shaking his head, Stanley returned to his seat with his second helping of food. When Sandra returned, he quickly swallowed his bite of food in order to thank her.

Sandra grinned. "You're welcome."

Stanley watched Sandra return to her chair. After pecking a kiss to Maggie's lips, she picked up her spoon and began eating again.

After finishing his second helping, Stanley relaxed back in his seat. He let out another sigh, fatigue weighing on him.

Stanley knew he should get off his butt and head home, but he needed just a moment's more rest.

Just when Stanley felt as if he had enough energy to rise, Nicholas and Bodb entered the room. He realized he had to be more tired than he thought to have missed their absence. Stanley would normally give his boss a report of the day during the end of the meal.

"Hi, Nicholas. Bodb," Stanley greeted with a dip of his chin. Noting the concern creasing his boss's features, he asked, "Everything all right?"

Stanley knew that, occasionally, Nicholas would struggle with clients or retailers in town due to being in an openly gay relationship. Fortunately, that had mostly died down over the years. Those in their county had grown accustomed to the fact.

It helped that Sheriff Archer Montgomery had ended up being mated to Bodb's youngest brother, Lludd. When Archer had come out, the current mayor—Sheldon Loreman—had had a fit. Especially when Archer had refused to employ Sheldon's bigoted son, Darcy. Sheldon had tried to get Archer sacked, but he'd only succeeded in getting himself booted, instead.

The mayor position was currently being handled by Archer himself, but he didn't care for the job. Elder Bodb was attempting to get the role filled by a paranormal. Unfortunately, other than those on the ranch, there were few paranormals in the area, and no one there was interested in dealing with politics, either.

"Everything's fine," Nicholas assured, his expression clearing. "I just feel a little bad because I'm probably going to be ruining most people's evening." He winced and offered a shrug. "At least, for a little while."

Arching a brow, Stanley asked, "What's going on?"

Nicholas indicated his gargoyle lover.

Bodb stood at the head of the table, and Nicholas quickly crossed to him.

"Can I have everyone's attention, please?" Elder Bodb asked, his deep voice carrying through the room without him having to raise his volume. Nearly instantly, all other conversation ceased. "Thank you." Bodb wrapped a thickly muscled, deep-purple arm around Nicholas's shoulders in a possessive hold. "Elder Gurrando is arriving tonight," Bodb told them. "I'll need everyone to assemble on the back deck for their arrival at ten-thirty."

Stanley winced before nodding once. He'd hoped to be asleep by then, and he knew the others helping him with branding were probably of the same mind.

"All of us, sir?" Keith asked. The older ranch hand looked confused. "If you don't mind my asking, why?" He shared a look with Walsh before glancing at Stanley and then returning his attention to the gargoyle elder. "Some of us are human." Then Keith rubbed his knee and offered a wry smile. "And need our rest to keep these old bones in line."

Keith was only in his mid-fifties, but ranch work could be tough on the body.

Elder Bodb offered Keith a commiserating smile. "I'm sorry, Keith. We shouldn't be keeping you long," he told him. "It's just a formality. The elder and the pair of enforcers with him need to see and scent everyone who lives here."

"That way, no one is mistakenly taken as a threat," Nicholas explained further. He patted Keith on the shoulder and smirked. "Enforcers can be protective of their elders."

Gladstone chuckled from where he sat at the table. He had his arm around his mate, Dayvid. "That we can be," he agreed amicably. Not only was the man Bodb's middle brother, but he was an enforcer for him, too. "Can't be too careful with our elders." The dark-brown gargoyle cocked his head. "I didn't think he was arriving until next week. Why the sudden change?"

Before Bodb could respond, Stanley slowly rose to his feet. "Please, excuse me," he murmured, picking up his dishes. "If I'm to be back here at ten-thirty, I'd really like to take my leave."

Not only did Stanley still need to get cleaned up, but he wanted to make the rounds of the barns one more time. Everything had been quiet when he'd finished earlier, but they had a mare that was due any day, as well as three heifers. Most births were in the spring, but it didn't always happen that way.

Besides, gargoyle politics didn't interest Stanley one iota — not unless it was going to somehow impact his duties, and he didn't think a visiting elder would do that. Stanley's job would be business as usual.

"Sure, Stanley," Nicholas responded with a smile. "See you in a couple of hours."

Stanley dipped his chin in acknowledgment before placing his dishes in a bin on a rolling cart near the sideboard. Then he headed out of the dining room. As Stanley slipped on his moccasins, he noticed Walsh and Keith following him.

"Later," Stanley murmured with a wave.

They responded in kind.

While they headed toward the bunkhouse, Stanley strode toward his cabin.

After a long hot shower, Stanley took a few minutes to rub the lotion on his sore upper arms and back. He sighed as whatever healing herbs Maggie put in it began to take effect. Stanley took a few minutes just to sit on the swing of his front porch in a pair of cargo shorts, enjoying the warm evening.

Considering the gargoyles ran around in loincloths, Stanley felt completely comfortable, and he knew no one would give him grief.

At ten after ten, Stanley slipped on a clean pair of moccasins and headed toward the foaling barn. He did a sweep, finding everything quiet. After leaving the barn, he crossed to the paddock containing the pregnant heifers. It was attached to an open-sided barn, but they usually only hung out in there during the heat of the day.

Stanley confirmed that everything was quiet there, too, before heading toward the back deck. He saw that nearly everyone had arrived. The sound of wings told Stanley that he was right on time.

After climbing the porch steps, Stanley turned and watched as forms appeared in the night sky. He noticed Keith slip from the back door, a tumbler in hand, and Walsh was jogging from the direction of the bunkhouse.

That's everyone, then.

Elder Bodb and Nicholas moved forward, watching the three shapes draw closer, the gargoyles appearing on the horizon. The form in the middle was dark-green with black horns and wings. The figure on the left was a medium-brown and also had black wings but no horns.

To Stanley's surprise, he found his attention riveted on the gargoyle on the right. The paranormal sported a light-gray hide with white wings and curling horns like a ram. He had the traditional thickly muscled frame and large body prevalent of an enforcer, and Stanley felt an odd desire to run his palms over the male.

Stanley quickly schooled his features and mentally squashed the notion. Getting his body under control was a little harder, but he did it, reminding himself that paranormals could smell arousal.

As they landed, Elder Bodb stepped forward and opened his mouth.

Before he could utter a word, the gray gargoyle's nostrils flared. His eyes widened just a smidge. He pinned his dark-gray-eyed gaze on Stanley and declared, "Mate."

Stanley gaped for a second before snapping his mouth shut. Taking a step backward, he hissed, "Well, shit."

CHAPTER TWO

That definitely wasn't the response Kultrak had dreamed of when meeting his mate. He knew from the report he'd read on all the people living at the ranch that they were aware of the paranormal world. With so many of those living there having already found their fated mate, surely the handsome Native American would understand the significance of it.

So why did he back up and curse?

Kultrak cleared his throat, doing his best to keep his features neutral. He damn well didn't want the man to realize how much that response concerned him. In truth, it hurt a little, too.

"Congratulations, Kultrak," Elder Gurrando rumbled, breaking the stunned silence that had fallen over the group. He clapped Kultrak on the upper back while offering him a wide smile. "What a blessed day."

The large deep-purple gargoyle that Kultrak knew was Elder Bodb cleared his throat. "Well, now." He glanced between Kultrak and the human he'd scented as his mate. "Uh, welcome to our home, Elder Gurrando. It's good to see you again," Bodb stated, sounding a little uncertain. "Will you introduce us to your enforcers?"

"Of course, Elder Bodb," Elder Gurrando began.

Elder Bodb lifted a claw-tipped hand, causing the other elder to pause and lift a dark-green eyebrow ridge in silent question. "If it's okay with you, can we drop the titles?" Bodb's smile turned wry. "We're not usually formal around here, and throwing all our titles around could get confusing

11

fast."

Elder Gurrando chuckled, resting his hands on his hips. "I'd like that." He reached out a hand. "Bodb?"

Bodb grinned and clasped Gurrando's hand, shaking it briefly. "Gurrando." Taking a step back, he returned his other arm to the man's shoulders who had to be his mate—Nicholas.

"With me today is Struano." Gurrando indicated the other enforcer. "And my old friend who's shocked us all is Kultrak."

Bodb nodded once. "This is my mate, Nicholas Lindson. He's kind enough to allow me to use his ranch as my base of operations." Pinning his human with a warm smile, Bodb rumbled, "Effectively turning his life upside-down."

"It was worth it," Nicholas responded with his own happy smile. Then he grinned and looked between Gurrando and Struano. "So, do either of you want to claim one of our other single men as your mate?" Nicholas teased. "They're all good men." Then he smirked as he peered to his left at a man with similar features, even if he did have dirty-blond hair instead of the dark-brown Nicholas sported. "Except my brother, Vernon, there. He's a pain in the ass."

"Ha, ha," Vernon muttered drily with a roll of his eyes.

Gurrando shook his head and sighed deeply. "Sadly, no. No one's scent calls to me." He looked at Struano. "You?"

Heaving his own sigh that sounded aggrieved, even if he was giving off a mild scent of humor, Struano shook his head. "Sadly, no." Then he pinned a heated look on Vernon. "Of course, that's not to say I wouldn't be open to a little fun."

Vernon's eyes widened even as a flush of color filled his cheeks.

Nicholas chuckled. "So I have all my hands assembled so you'd be familiar with their face and scent." He waved a hand to indicate all the men — and the two women who were cuddled on a lounge chair, one heavy with child — and claimed, "If you need anything, they'll be happy to help with most things." Turning to peer at the human that Kultrak desperately wanted to touch, Nicholas stated, "And the one I'm certain you're most interested in is my ranch foreman, Stanley Redfeather." Nicholas's brows furrowed, and his eyes narrowed as he cocked his head just a little. "And Stanley will have to speak for himself in regards to his reaction."

Stanley's chest expanded as he took in a deep breath. Wearing only a pair of cargo shorts and a set of moccasins, there was a whole lot of lean muscle on display, making Kultrak's mouth water. The man thrust a hand through his long black hair, pushing it away from his face.

"I apologize for my knee-jerk reaction, uh, Kultrak," Stanley murmured, his soft tenor like a caress to Kultrak's senses. "I've seen how . . . swiftly paranormals like to move in regards to bonding with their mates, and I—" Stanley paused, his black brows furrowing as he shook his head. "I don't want to offend you, but I don't think I can give that to you. Not the way you probably hope."

Kultrak mulled that over in his mind for a few heartbeats, hating that their first moments together were so public. "I . . . ask only for a chance," he began, struggling with what to say. "To get to know you."

Stanley appeared relieved, and he nodded. "A chance, I can give."

Relieved that he'd said something right, Kultrak smiled at the man he intended to soon claim.

Not that I'll tell him that. He seems . . . skittish.

Kultrak wondered why. With so many paired with paranormals at the ranch, surely he knew the pleasures, commitment, and safety that bonding would bring. Kultrak decided he would have to reiterate the benefits.

Before Kultrak could add a word, Stanley opened his

mouth in a wide yawn. He lifted his hand and covered his mouth, even as a hint of color filled his bronzed cheeks.

"Sorry," Stanley muttered once he was finished. After sliding his tongue over his full bottom lip, he admitted, "It's been a long day, and I have another long one planned for tomorrow." Rubbing the back of his neck with one hand, Stanley held Kultrak's gaze as he stated, "I know you're here as a guard for your elder as he has his meeting. I think . . . it may be best if you take care of that while I head to bed."

The wiry human tried to appear as if he were offering understanding that Kultrak was there to work as opposed to what he seemed to actually be doing—running away.

Kultrak was about to ask Gurrando for a short reprieve. After all, his elder hadn't been lying when he'd called him an old friend. He'd been Gurrando's right-hand man for several centuries, and his friend would be happy for him and do his best to accommodate him, regardless of the troubling reason for them being there.

"I know you think I'm running away," Stanley commented astutely, taking a step toward him. "I'm really not." Then he yawned again with a shake of his head. "This'll give me a chance to wrap my head around it," Stanley told him. "I'll still be here tomorrow evening after you wake, and we can talk then."

Deciding to take his mate at his word, Kultrak nodded once. "If that is your wish." As much as he wanted to wrap his arms around Stanley and hold him as he slept, just to be close to him, he'd promised to give the human time. "May I walk you to your room?"

Stanley hesitated. After a quick glance around, he refocused on Kultrak. "To my cabin." He indicated behind Kultrak and to the left to a small structure about a hundred paces away with a cozy-looking swing on the front porch.

"Thank you." Kultrak didn't think it would be nearly

enough time with his newly found mate, but he would take what he could get. After getting a nod from Gurrando, Kultrak turned and indicated the cabin. "Shall we?"

Sweeping a gaze over the assembled group, who all seemed to be continuing to watch them with interest, Stanley cleared his throat before muttering, "Night." Then he took the steps and started toward the indicated cabin.

Kultrak turned and quickly fell into step beside him. Several called good nights behind them, and from the corner of Kultrak's eyes, he noticed plenty of people moving. Many of them headed toward the bunkhouse, while a few slipped into the house.

With Kultrak's heightened hearing, he easily made out Bodb telling someone, "Sindrid, will you hang out just inside and guide Kultrak to the lounge after he returns?"

"Of course, sir," a deep voice replied.

"Please join us, Gurrando," Bodb encouraged, and the sound of people moving filled the air.

Then Kultrak dismissed those behind him in favor of focusing on his mate. "Thank you for giving me a few moments, Stanley," he murmured, keeping his voice low enough to offer a hint of intimacy even though they were probably still being watched. "I understand it can be difficult for humans to simply accept the word of a stranger that they'll be perfect for each other."

Stanley scoffed softly, offering a single nod. "That's definitely part of it." Pausing at the bottom of the steps, he turned to face him while shoving his hands into the pockets of his cargo shorts. "The other problem is, my life is here, Kultrak. This is what I've trained to do since I was old enough to walk." His expression turned pained as he slowly panned his gaze over the dark ranch. Stanley's voice came out a whisper as he asked, "Where do you call home, Kultrak?"

"Currently, the Smokey Mountains in Tennessee," Kultrak

admitted, seeing part of Stanley's problem. "And I wouldn't expect you to make all the compromises."

Unable to resist his need to touch any longer, Kultrak reached out and gripped Stanley's right forearm. As he gently tugged his mate's limb from his pocket, he felt the tension under the flesh. Doing his best to ignore the ripple of awareness that flooded his body at such a simple touch while threading the fingers of one of his hands with Stanley's, Kultrak had to remind Stanley of something important.

"You must know that part of the way a gargoyle is wired is to please our mate, right?" Kultrak told him, gently massaging his human's palm. "Your happiness in a location to live is a big part of that."

Kultrak knew that asking Stanley to give up his life wasn't fair, no matter how often he'd seen humans do it for other paranormals over the centuries.

I have a lot to think about, too.

With a soft grunt, Stanley nodded once more with narrowed eyes. "Okay. Uh, I'll see you tomorrow, then," he told him, tugging at his hand lightly.

Unable to let him go just yet, Kultrak tightened his hold while lifting his free hand. He moved slowly, carefully gauging his seemingly skittish human's reactions. While Stanley tensed, he didn't pull away, so Kultrak finished the move and cradled his mate's strong jaw.

"I'll leave you to your evening, Stanley," Kultrak rumbled. Bending, he focused on Stanley's lips, making his intention clear. "After I taste you. May I?"

Kultrak would never take what Stanley wouldn't freely give. To that end, he paused with his face inches from his human's. Shifting his focus to Stanley's dark eyes, Kultrak peered into their depths . . . waiting.

Stanley's nostrils flared, and his jaw clenched once under Kultraks' hold. After several heartbeats, his human licked his lips once, twice. Then Stanley nodded nearly infinitesimally.

Kultrak accepted the permission. Lowering his head the rest of the way, he sealed his lips over Stanley's. With a gentle swipe along his bottom lip, Kultrak took his first taste of his forever love.

Stanley's flavor burst across Kultrak's taste buds—robust and masculine. A nip to the human's bottom lip caused his mate to open to him, and he eased his tongue a little into Stanley's parted lips. His human's flavor intensified, and unable to help himself, Kultrak let out a soft moan.

Instead of doing as he desperately wanted and ravishing his human, Kultrak kept the contact light. He teased at Stanley's tongue, who immediately responded by pressing his tongue back against him. Kultrak reveled in Stanley's response, pleased his mate wasn't passive, but kissing back and doing a little tasting of his own.

With his cock throbbing and his body flushed with arousal, Kultrak eased the kiss to an end. He took in Stanley's flushed face and wet, swollen lips. His human's dark eyes appeared to be black liquid pools filled with desire, and Kultrak wished he could follow up on what his mate's body seemed to be telling him.

Except, Kultrak knew pushing now would set him back more than he could ever gain.

As Kultrak slid his thumb along Stanley's jawline, slowly releasing his face, he pressed one more kiss to the corner of his mate's mouth. "I look forward to getting to know you, Stanley," Kultrak whispered as he straightened. With a squeeze to Stanley's hand that he still held, he added, "Have pleasant dreams, my mate."

Stanley's nostrils flared as he took in a sharp breath. He cleared his throat as he pulled away. "Uh, yeah. You, too." Then he grunted and shook his head. "I mean, good luck with your meeting."

With that reminder of his job, Kultrak smiled and released

him. "Thank you." He took a step backward, but he couldn't get himself to move further.

Stanley licked his lips as he roved his gaze over Kultrak for a few seconds. Then he seemed to shake himself out of the lustful stupor Kultrak's kiss had pulled him into. He smiled faintly, nodded, then headed up the stairs.

Pleasure filled Kultrak when Stanley paused in the doorway to peer at him for a few seconds before disappearing into his cabin.

Kultrak grinned as he turned and headed toward the main lodge. After adjusting his erection behind his loincloth, he headed into the house. A large brown gargoyle waited for him, so Kultrak assumed he was Sindrid.

"Congratulations," Sindrid told him with a smile. "Stanley's a fantastic catch." Then he sobered and warned, "Just remember, this is his home, and we are his family." He began leading the way through the house. "You do anything to harm him, and you'll answer to us."

"He's my mate," Kultrak reminded the other gargoyle. Frowning, he declared, "There's no way I'd hurt him."

"There are more ways to hurt a person than physically," Sindrid countered. Then he revealed, "I don't know all the details, but I know Stanley's been burned before. It's made him gun-shy."

Kultrak had guessed as much. "I'll give him all the time he needs," he vowed.

Sindrid nodded once before knocking on the right side of a pair of sliding doors.

Hearing Bodb call for them to enter, Kultrak did his best to, for the moment anyway, put his mate out of his mind.

CHAPTER THREE

Stanley didn't sleep for shit. His dreams were flooded with a confusing mix of memory and fantasy. He woke to the harsh words spoken by Casey, the last man he'd dared to try a relationship with. Instead of Casey's tenor, though, Stanley heard Casey saying how he never made enough time for him in Kultrak's deep sultry voice, how he would imagine it sounding hard from anger.

The glow of the nearly full moon streamed through Stanley's windows as he eased to the side of the bed. He checked the time on the clock, seeing that, as usual, he'd woken before his alarm. Although, this time around, Stanley had a good thirty minutes before needing to get up.

Knowing it would be pointless to try to go back to sleep, Stanley pushed from the bed and his rumpled sheets. He blinked slowly, trying to get his eyes to stop the fatigue sting. Skipping turning on the bathroom light, Stanley used the glow to navigate.

Stanley rested a hand on the back of the toilet as he eased his morning bladder. After washing his hands, he brushed his teeth before grabbing another brush and making quick work of clearing the tangles from his butt-length hair. With his eyes nearly closed, Stanley braided his hair into an intricate plait to keep it out of his way while working. After tying it off, the braid just reaching the middle of his back. Stanley bent and splashed water on his face . . . several times . . . trying to get his mind in order.

Instead, the only thought that kept repeating through his

brain was the fact that it was still dark outside. The sun would probably be up in less than twenty minutes, but that was enough time to say good morning to Kultrak. He shook his head at the wayward idea.

Geez, I am not some love-struck teenager.

After dressing, Stanley headed toward the front door. He slipped his bare feet into his moccasins and paused on the front porch. Tipping his chin up, Stanley gazed toward the pale light in the east, heralding the rising sun.

As a light breeze blew across Stanley's cheeks, he found his gaze straying to the large horse barn on his right. The place housed their younger horses that were still in training, but that wasn't what drew his attention. Instead, Stanley knew that the loft had been converted into a safe place for the gargoyles to roost.

Originally, when Bodb had first moved to the ranch, there had been a number of gargoyles forced into their stone statue form during the daylight hours, so that was where they did it. While all the gargoyles living on the ranch had mated, they still needed a place to safely roost. As Stanley understood it, their stone statue form was similar to a human's REM sleep, and they needed to indulge in it for at least an hour or two a week in order to stay healthy.

The barn's hay loft door stood open, and Stanley spotted a hulking figure silhouetted against the darkness. He didn't know why, but he felt certain the male was Kultrak. Lifting a hand, Stanley offered a silent morning greeting.

The figure returned the wave, and something warm swam through Stanley's veins. He was once again tempted to go see the gargoyle. Glancing back to the east, Stanley tried to decide just how much time he could manage with the male.

Another figure appearing beside Kultrak's nixed the idea. Kultrak nodded and disappeared within before the second male closed the door.

Feeling as if he'd missed out on something, Stanley

stepped off his porch and headed to the main house for break-fast.

Pulling his hat from his head, Stanley used the bandana in his other hand to wipe his brow. He shoved the cloth square into his back pocket as he plopped his hat back on his head. Stanley did his best to ignore the sweat-dampened fabric against his forehead.

Stanley snagged the water bottle from the satchel on his horse's left side and brought it to his lips. As he guzzled several deep swallows, he enjoyed the fresh taste. While the water was no longer cold, it still felt fantastic as it slid down his throat.

After returning the bottle to his bag, Stanley rested his hands on the horn as he surveyed the paddocks and the men within wrangling cows for branding. He felt his horse's heavy breathing beneath his legs, and he knew he'd stayed in the corral a little longer than he should have before swapping out with another hand. Working, however, allowed him to keep his focus on something other than Kultrak.

The deep-gray-hided male was never far from Stanley's thoughts. He had heard that the human half of a pairing felt the pull, too, but he'd underestimated just how strong the feeling would be. Stanley had thought he would be able to continue with his life as usual until he was ready to deal with the gargoyle's declaration.

That was proving difficult.

His horse's movement beneath him caught Stanley's attention, and he chuckled as the horse dipped his muzzle into the water trough Stanley had stopped them at. His horse swished his nose forward and back in the water, causing it to splash around him. The horse coated his front legs and chest in the spray before settling in for a drink.

Stanley returned his attention to the corral just in time to see a bull-calf charge at Walsh. The hand jumped to the left and grabbed the fence, pulling himself to safety. However, the move hadn't been necessary since Keith threw his lariat swiftly and accurately and lassoed the calf, jerking it to a stop three feet from Walsh and the fence.

Walsh recovered instantly and jumped back to the ground. He grabbed the fighting calf's legs and used his momentum to flip him to his back. With deft moves, Walsh tied the calf's legs, immobilizing it.

Virgil was there a second later with the branding iron. In less than a minute, the task was done, and the group released the animal. Keith used his horse to herd the bawling calf to the exit on the other side of the paddock where Lebone — a mated gargoyle currently in human form — manned the gate, releasing the animal into the herd of those already branded.

Stanley eased from his horse's back. He used one rein to lead him a little to the right. After grabbing a rope already tied to the hitching post, he clipped it to the horse's halter. His horse could rest while he took a turn on the ground.

Grabbing the water bottle again, Stanley crossed to the fence. "You okay there, Walsh?" he called, taking a sip of his drink.

He appreciated that Lebone's mate, Pauline, chose bottled water with electrolytes already added. With how sweaty they all became during fall branding, they lost plenty of minerals. Getting them replenished right away helped them recover more swiftly.

"I'm still good, boss," Walsh replied with a grin. The younger man's brown eyes twinkled. "Don't forget to stretch those old legs of yours while you watch."

Stanley rolled his eyes as he scoffed. "Youngsters think they're so funny," he muttered, although he appreciated that Walsh felt comfortable enough with them to offer a ribbing.

In truth, Walsh was over a decade younger than Stanley's

forty-two years, but he was a good hand. He still had some learning to do with training the horses, but he had great cow instincts. While Virgil occasionally missed a sign and ended up kicked, Walsh seemed to always be a step ahead of the cows.

Still, Stanley took Walsh's advice. He didn't want to stiffen up while he was supposed to be recovering. With that thought in mind, he lifted a moccasin-clad foot to the bottom rail of the fence and began stretching.

Stanley watched the group for another fifteen minutes before Walsh took a rest. Virgil took his place while Stanley handled the branding irons. He knew a lot of places that had transitioned into tags, but Nicholas's father had refused due to the transition cost. When Nicholas took over, they'd discussed it, but they hadn't taken the plunge, yet.

Maybe someday.

After branding the third cow, Stanley spotted Nicholas striding toward the paddock. He was dressed in his work clothes, heralding that he intended to join in. That was another huge difference between Baltus and Nicholas—Nicholas worked the ranch—Baltus had been a lawyer in town and had merely been a figurehead.

"Morning, Nicholas," Stanley greeted, tipping his hat at his boss. "You look ready to get your hands dirty."

Nicholas grinned, his dark-brown eyes twinkling. "Yep, and it's afternoon now." He pointed toward the sun. "I'm also here to help ya'll start taking your lunch breaks. Pauline will be out with a hell of a spread in about ten minutes."

Stanley grinned, and he knew he wasn't the only one. At the mention of food, his stomach growled. His mouth also watered, and anticipation filled him.

Evidently, Stanley wasn't the only one who became distracted by the mention of lunch. Biscane—the gargoyle at the gate used to allow a calf into the paddock—cursed as he was jostled sideways. Several playing calves had hit the gate, making it swing open. Even as Biscane pushed the gate closed, obviously using his paranormal strength to shove against the large animals, several managed to slip through.

Nicholas—who had been in the process of hopping the fence—landed right in the path of one of the charging animals.

Cursing, Stanley leaped sideways. He pushed Nicholas out of the large calf's path and twisted, trying to do the same. The animal tossed its head, hooking him with a horn as it passed. Pain stabbed through his side, yanking a gasp from Stanley's lungs.

Stanley felt his body spinning, but he couldn't seem to stop it. Falling, he landed hard on his back. For a second, he froze with the wind knocked from his lungs as pain caused his limbs to freeze.

Spotting the calf as it pivoted, lowered its head, and charged at him again, Stanley forced himself to roll out of the animal's path. A second later, the calf bawled as it was lifted into the air by Biscane. In his massive black frame, the gargoyle easily hefted the animal and carried it out of the paddock and into another smaller one.

"Shit, Stanley," Nicholas muttered, dropping to his knees beside him. "I owe you one, man."

Stanley shook his head as he began to push to a sitting position. "Naw. It's a ranch," he murmured, doing his best to breathe through the pain. "Shit happens."

"Stay down, Stanley," Virgil ordered from where he knelt on his other side. "We need to see how bad it is."

Stanley growled in annoyance. Although he couldn't fight against both men's firm hands. "I'm fine," he insisted, reaching out to push Virgil's hands away with one hand while pressing the other to his hurting side. "Just a scratch."

"Not likely," Walsh stated, appearing with the first aid kit.

They always kept one handy while working with the cattle. "Little too much blood for that, boss-man."

Making the mistake of looking at his side, Stanley saw exactly what the others were looking at. His shirt had been torn open, and he could see the gash from between the blood-soaked fabric. His life-fluid seeped from the wound, dripping down his side and soaking into the dirt of the paddock ground.

Stanley jerked his gaze away as black spots danced across his vision. While he wasn't normally squeamish about the sight of blood—after all, he'd helped many a heifer during a problem birth—there was something different about seeing his own blood pouring from him. Sucking in a sharp breath, Stanley let it out through pursed lips.

"Aww, shit, man," Biscane muttered, landing nearby. "I'm so sorry."

"It's fine," Stanley insisted. "Not your fault."

"Uh, yeah, it was," Biscane claimed, shaking his head. "I'm the one who fumbled the damn gate."

"Shit happens," Stanley repeated, shaking his head. He stopped the movement when spots immediately flashed across his vision. "I'll heal." Then Stanley smirked up at the worried-looking gargoyle—*when did I lie back down?* "Just means you gotta do more branding work while I kick back for a day."

"This is gonna take more than a day, Stanley," Nicholas murmured, squeezing his hand. Stanley focused on his boss, uncertain when the other man had picked it up. Nicholas stared at him with worried brown eyes. "You're going to need stitches. Lebone is calling for an ambulance."

"No." Stanley shook his head. "I don't need—"

"I'll tell you what you need until you can think straight again," Nicholas demanded. "And that's the hospital and stitches."

Stanley growled softly, glaring at Nicholas's fierce expression even though he looked a little pale. "Can't someone do it here?" he asked. "Don't wanna leave." When Nicholas opened his mouth, obviously intending to deny him, Stanley added, "We've stitched up animals a-plenty."

"This is different," Virgil told him, drawing his attention. The other man pressed a gauze pad against his side, sending fiery tendrils of pain through Stanley's torso. "I don't know if the horn cut into your muscle. Plus, with all the dirt, debris, and possible contamination from first a horn, then the dirt of the arena, I don't think we should risk it."

Stanley really didn't want to agree, but his friends made sense.

"An ambulance is on the way," Lebone claimed, easing to one knee. "Hang in there, Stanley."

Blinking slowly, Stanley realized his vision was beginning to fade. Unspeakable agony coursed through him, and his side had begun to go numb. Virgil had maneuvered himself into a position where Stanley couldn't see his side while he and Walsh worked on it.

"Son, do as you're told," Keith ordered, his deep voice soft with reassurance. "There's no shame in getting medical help."

"Not about shame," Stanley claimed, surprised to find his voice coming out in a whisper. *Damn.* "T-Tell Kultrak sorry."

Those were his last words before Stanley lost his battle with darkness.

CHAPTER FOUR

U pon waking from roost, even before Kultrak opened his eyes, he found himself smiling. The image of Stanley's strong, handsome form seemed superimposed on the backs of his eyelids. Kultrak couldn't help the way his body reacted to the stunning image.

My mate. I'll get to spend time with my mate.

Kultrak's body reacted predictably to the memory of Stanley's scent, the feel of his skin under his palms, and the exquisite flavor of his lips. Except, then the smell of trepidation and unease teased his nostrils. Kultrak snapped his eyes open and swept his gaze around the secluded space in the loft where they'd been shown to roost.

Spotting the cots spread out around the hay-hidden space, Kultrak once again mentally scoffed at the silliness of the items . . . as thoughtful as it was. After all, they were stone statues. It wasn't like they could feel their comfort, no matter how nice.

Noticing both Gurrando and Struano already on their feet, their attention on Bodb, Nicholas, Lebone, and Sindrid, Kultrak quickly rose, as well. He took in their tense features and worried expressions. The men were clearly upset about something.

"What is it, Bodb?" Gurrando asked, moving toward the other elder. "Have you heard anything regarding Laagstine or Rayzon?"

With Elder Bodb having mated several years before, plus having connections with a couple of gargoyle clutches, as well as other paranormal groups, he had resources that some elders did not. On top of that, Bodb had always been known to have a fantastic grasp of changing times. He easily hid amongst the human world, even when he hadn't had a human form.

Considering that, when certain rumors had reached Gurrando, he'd chosen to seek Bodb's help. That was what the meeting the evening before had been about.

Gurrando had explained that Elder Laagstine had gone to visit Elder Rayzon, and that had been the last time anyone had heard from Rayzon. At first, Laagstine had claimed that was a coincidence. However, it didn't take long for the elder to suddenly disappear as well.

When a number of Circle Enforcers searched both elders' estates, there had been plenty of questionable evidence in a hidden room in Laagstine's home — information indicating his prejudice against humans, even going so far as calling other paranormal species as *lesser*. The gargoyle elder had a secret account with plenty of mysterious deposits and expenses. Some were easily seen as bribe and blackmail payments, but many were not so clear-cut.

Elder Gurrando had conferred with Elder Vermidian in Wyoming, as well as Elder Korsair in Virginia. They'd agreed to share the information with Elder Bodb. They weren't certain if any of the other elders could be involved, but considering he was mated with a human and lived amongst paranormals of many species, they all agreed that Bodb couldn't be.

They'd been right.

The prior evening, after they'd shared their evidence with Bodb, the large gargoyle had been livid. He'd agreed to reach out through his contacts. They'd also made plans to start reaching out and getting a feel for the remaining elders. If they weren't involved, for safety's sake, they even discussed them using Bodb and Nicholas's ranch as a home base . . . for the time being anyway.

I can't wait to share that with Stanley. He'll appreciate knowing that we'll be staying here for the foreseeable future.

"Afraid I haven't heard anything about either of them yet," Bodb admitted, grimacing. "Although I have sent a couple of my people to their estates to do a little snooping of their own."

"Then what's happened?" Gurrando asked, glancing between the men. "We can tell something's up."

When Nicholas rubbed Bodb's upper arm in a soothing way before focusing on Kultrak, Kultrak felt his gut begin to churn. "Stanley?" he whispered, unable to help jumping to conclusions. "Did he run?"

Nicholas quickly shook his head. "No," he stated firmly. "He didn't run." After a glance between the other gargoyles, the human told him, "There was an accident during branding today." Nicholas's lips pinched, and he furrowed his brown brows. "Stanley was injured while saving me from getting hurt."

"Injured," Kultrak whispered, a mixture of disbelief and denial flooding him. "H-How badly? What happened?" Then he realized that wasn't even the most important thing. "Where is he?"

"Stanley's home, in bed," Nicholas quickly told him, lifting a hand in placation. "He's—Shit. Kultrak, wait!"

As soon as Kultrak had heard Stanley's location, he'd lunged to the top of the hay bale wall. He quickly crawled across the top, then dropped to the loft floor. Kultrak had just reached the loft door and slid the wooden slider open when he felt a hand on his shoulder.

With a snarl, Kultrak turned toward whoever dared to try to stop him from going to his mate. Upon seeing Gurrando's look of understanding, he sobered.

"Please, don't try to stop me," Kultrak rumbled, not wanting to go against his best friend and elder. "I need to see him."

"None of us will stop you from seeing your mate, Kultrak,"

Gurrando assured him. Giving Kultrak's shoulder a squeeze, his elder reminded him, "We'll all be here for you and him, but perhaps you should at least hear what his injuries are before going to him." Gurrando stared at him intently. "After all, you don't want to accidentally hurt him in your exuberance."

Letting out a deep sigh, Kultrak nodded. "I see the wisdom in your words." That didn't make it any easier to focus once more on the others rather than fly out the loft door to seek out his injured mate. Still, he managed to ask again, "What happened?"

"He saved me from getting gored when several yearlings got loose in the paddock we were working in," Nicholas explained, rubbing the back of his neck. "But couldn't quite get out of the way himself. One caught his side just right with a horn."

"The impact caused Stanley to spin," Lebone explained, picking up the explanation. "That pulled the horn back out, tearing part of his side at the same time. We called an ambulance, and they took him to emergency." The brown gargoyle offered an encouraging smile. "It looks bad right now. Seventy-eight stitches. But he'll make a full recovery."

Sindrid nodded, his smile a little crooked. "The biggest concern is infection, but just think, if you bond, the chance of that will be slim." He even winked.

"I promised Stanley time," Kultrak mumbled, even though he'd immediately thought the same thing. It would speed up the healing, too. "I have to give him that."

No matter what.

Grimacing, Sindrid nodded once more. "Well, then we'll explain how to care for him, and we'll be there for him when you can't be."

Kultrak glanced between the guys, taking in their understanding and encouraging expressions. "Thank you."

"Well, then," Bodb rumbled, indicating the open loft door. "Stanley's front door is unlocked. Biscane is currently sitting with him." Wrapping his arm around Nicholas's waist, the elder told him, "I will forever be grateful for Stanley's quick action. He's family, and we take care of family."

Kultrak nodded once more. "Thank you." He appreciated that Stanley had people watching out for him.

"Go to him, Kultrak," Gurrando urged, patting his shoulder. With an encouraging smile, he waved toward Struano. "Between Struano and Bodb's people, I'm perfectly safe. Go take care of your mate."

Planning to do exactly that, Kultrak turned back to the open door. He jumped from the loft door and spread his wings. Easily catching his weight, Kultrak glided through the air, beating his wings once, twice, to pick up speed.

In just a few seconds, Kultrak landed before the porch he'd left the evening before. He took the four steps two at a time. Kultrak grabbed the handle of the door, hesitating just an instant, his heart beating wildly in his chest.

My injured mate is inside. Gotta stay in control.

No matter how much Kultrak wanted to push the possibility of bonding, he knew he couldn't take advantage of the situation. He needed to keep himself in check. Something told him that Stanley wouldn't appreciate being manipulated in that way.

With that thought firmly in mind, Kultrak turned the knob and headed inside. The first thing that hit him was the robust smell of his mate permeating the place . . . and nearly no one else's. Kultrak loved the knowledge that his mate lived alone, and evidently, he rarely allowed others into his space.

Gonna change that fast.

Taking into consideration the fact that Bodb had told him that Stanley was sleeping, Kultrak resisted the urge to call out. He took in the open concept, cabin-like interior decorated clearly in a Native American style. There were crossed hatchets hanging over the stone fireplace that looked usable as opposed to ceremonial. Pottery rested on the mantel, as well as a large knife in a sheath. The faint smell of woodsmoke hung in the air, telling him that Stanley enjoyed using his fireplace often.

That'll be nice. I love marshmallows.

While most wouldn't expect it, and Kultrak didn't advertise it, he had a bit of a sweet tooth.

There were several doors in the cabin. Two stood open, revealing a room set up as an office as well as a bedroom. From within the bedroom, he heard rustling.

Kultrak started that way, concern riding him. If his injured mate was thrashing, he could hurt himself further. He needed to make certain he was resting comfortably.

He hoped that just his presence or maybe a gentle touch would allow his mate to do that.

Just as Kultrak reached the doorway, he spotted a large form moving within. He curled his lip in a snarl as the scent of Biscane registered. It looked as if the large gargoyle was adjusting Stanley's blankets, and a surge of jealousy rushed through Kultrak.

That's my job.

Obviously registering Kultrak's growl, Biscane snapped his head up. His expression when Biscane spotted Kultrak was one of guilt. He cringed as he backed away from Stanley.

Kultrak backed up a step, allowing Biscane to pass him. Knowing his response was irrational—after all, Biscane was a mated gargoyle just helping out a friend—he muttered, "Thank you for caring for Stanley while I could not."

To Kultrak's surprise, Biscane ducked his head as he mumbled, "The least I could do. My fault, after all."

Cocking his head, Kultrak frowned at the hulking black gargoyle. "What are you talking about?" The others hadn't said anything like that.

"I let the gate slip," Biscane claimed. When Kultrak just stared at him in confusion, the other male elaborated, "I was manning the gate, allowing the cows into the branding paddock. I got distracted, and when tussling cows slammed into the gate, I let it slip, allowing four of them in the paddock at once." Remorse filled Biscane's eyes and tone as he rubbed the back of his neck. "If I'd been paying more attention, Stanley wouldn't have gotten hurt."

"Biscane, it was an accident," Nicholas stated from near the front door. He wasn't alone, and Kultrak hadn't even realized they'd arrived. When Biscane still didn't look convinced, Nicholas continued, "Accidents happen on a ranch. If a human had been manning the gate, no way would they have been able to hold it closed against the force of four yearlings slamming into it." Shaking his head, the ranch owner crossed to Biscane and rested a hand on the big gargoyle's upper arm. "It was an accident, and even Stanley already told ya so."

Upon hearing the firmly spoken words again, Biscane seemed to deflate. "Just feel damn guilty, is all."

"Well, don't." Stanley's slightly slurred words carried from inside the bedroom. "Accident." Moaning softly, he mumbled thickly, "Whud they give me?"

Kultrak rushed into Stanley's bedroom, hurrying to the bedside table. The space was illuminated by a small nightstand light, casting his mate in a halo. It was still enough to showcase Stanley's pale skin and heavy-lidded, dilated eyes — and not for the reason Kultrak would have wished.

Unable to help himself, Kultrak settled into the chair by the bed and gripped his mate's hand. He felt the slight clamminess on his mate's skin and wished he could take away his human's pain. Kultrak gently massaged Stanley's long fingers, hoping to soothe him a little.

"You ended up with seventy-eight stitches, Stanley," Nicholas reminded from where he'd slipped to the foot of the bed.

"You'll be on some pretty heavy pain meds for a couple of days."

"Days." Stanley's black brows furrowed, expressing his distaste. "Be fine tomorrow."

"No, you really won't," Nicholas countered, sounding a little amused. "You won't be able to move with those stitches in your side. You're on bed rest for at least two days, and we'll talk about minimal movement after that."

Stanley turned his head and smiled wanly at Kultrak. "We could bond," he suggested softly. "That'd speed up my healing. Right?"

Kultrak wanted to agree. His cock perked up just at the idea. Except, he knew his mate was drugged up and in pain. He wasn't thinking properly. Kultrak refused to take advantage of him in that way.

Leaning close, Kultrak whispered, "In a few days, when you're thinking a little more clearly, I would love to bond with you, my mate." When Stanley scowled, blinking slowly, Kultrak had the funny feeling that his human was going to try to counter him in some way. Unwilling to allow his soon-to-be lover to try to sway him — because he knew he would want to do anything to please his mate — Kultrak leaned forward and pecked a kiss to Stanley's lips, silencing him. When he eased back again, he reminded him, "You asked for a little time so we can get to know each other. We'll still do that. It'll just be in here, that's all."

"Kultrak is right, Stanley," Bodb rumbled softly. "If that's still what you want in a couple of days, you know he'll do anything for you." He smiled in encouragement. "Take advantage of the downtime, Stanley. You work too hard."

Stanley grunted before letting out a long sigh. Taking in the way his mate's long black lashes rested on his cheeks, his eyes closed once more, Kultrak realized his human had passed back out. Worry filling him, he focused on the group lurking just inside the doorway.

"He's fine, Kultrak," Nicholas assured. "Sleep is good for him right now." Indicating the bed, he offered, "Why don't we go get you food and drink? That way, you can stay here with him." Leaning against Bodb, who instantly slipped an arm around his waist, Nicholas added, "I'll bring some bone broth in a thermos, too. You can help him drink a little the next time he wakes. He'll be ready for another pain pill, too."

"In about three hours, his bandages will need to be changed, and there's some ointment to put on the stitches," Biscane told him from where he leaned against the doorframe. "I'll show you how. The doc explained it to us while Stanley was sleeping before he was released."

Kultrak nodded. "Thank you," he rumbled, suddenly feeling grateful to be surrounded by these men. "I'd appreciate that."

Stanley's family . . . and now . . . perhaps mine, too.

Kultrak couldn't say he minded. While it was trouble that had brought them to Bodb's door, he knew it was with Fate's blessing.

CHAPTER FIVE

The pain pulsing through his side pushed into Stanley's mind, rousing him from an oddly comfortable sleep-state. Breathing deeply, he tried to get the discomfort pulsing through him under control. Stanley also tried to get his muddled brain to tell him why he'd been feeling so comfortable.

Feeling a heavy weight draped over the left side of his body confused Stanley. So did the warm hard frame pressing against that same side. The limb resting on Stanley's chest finally registered, and he snapped his eyelids open.

Stanley turned his head and couldn't help but gape. Kultrak lay beside him on the bed, his big body surprisingly warm, considering he was a creature of stone. Just that fast, Stanley mentally rolled his eyes. He'd touched a gargoyle in their natural form before—their hand or arm while working—and they'd always been an average temperature.

Then Stanley found his attention moving to the weight draped over most of his body, and he nearly gaped. It was Kultrak's deep gray wing spread over him as if to offer protection and warmth. Stanley's fingers itched to touch as he'd never had the opportunity before.

Stanley knew that a gargoyle didn't appreciate the average touch to their wings. The appendages were sensitive. Only lovers touched the billowy folds, which he'd been told felt like the most buttery-soft leather. Stanley had also seen the gargoyles use them as weapons while fighting just like the claws on their hands and feet, and he appreciated that he'd never been on the receiving end of a gargoyle's powerful wing-strikes.

Resisting the urge, Stanley slid his focus up Kultrak's wing to his arm, where it rested on his chest. The male's light-gray hide bulged with muscles, even while relaxed, and he wanted to trace each ridge and dip with his tongue. When Stanley turned his attention to Kultrak's face, he sucked in a sharp breath upon finding the big male's deep gray eyes staring right back at him.

"Um, hey," Stanley mumbled lamely. He hoped Kultrak would chalk the flush on his cheeks up to his injury as opposed to the embarrassment he felt. "Uh, guess it's nighttime."

"It is," Kultrak rumbled deeply. Gently, he scratched his clawed hand over Stanley's chest in a surprisingly soft caress. "You ready for some bone broth? Your friends brought it a couple of hours ago in a thermos." Kultrak swept his gaze over Stanley's features as if searching for something. "You also need something in your stomach before taking another pain pill."

At the mention of the pain pill, a memory pushed into Stanley's mind. "I woke up before, didn't I?"

"Yes."

The images were hazy, but he was sure Biscane had needed reassurance — *damn gargoyle thinks my injury is his fault.* Stanley recalled reassuring him. Then something else flicked through his mind.

Snapping his gaze to Kultrak's intense gray eyes, Stanley whispered, "I asked, uh, offered, um, to bond?"

Kultrak's lips curved into just the smallest of smiles as he dipped his chin in a nod. "You did." Before Stanley could ask the question — and even as he clenched his ass, trying to sense if he felt any different — Kultrak continued, "And just as I promised to give you time, we'll revisit the subject in a couple of days." Grimacing, the gargoyle muttered, "When you're not hopped up on pain meds and feeling a little confused."

Letting out a deep sigh, Stanley murmured, "Thank you." Grimacing, he admitted, "And now I feel like an ass that I'd even think you'd do that while I'm mostly out of it."

Lifting one shoulder in a half-shrug, Kultrak rumbled, "You don't know me. Maybe I could have been that type of asshole." He skimmed his hand up and teased his claws along Stanley's jawline, sending a trickle of goose bumps down his neck and over his shoulders. "Plus, gargoyles are wired to please our mates. I want you happy." With a wry smile, Kultrak added, "I just happened to realize that *that* wouldn't have made you happy. Not really."

Stanley let out a relieved breath as he smiled gratefully at the gargoyle. "Thank you." Then he tried to shift his weight, causing a shard of pain to lance through his side. Growling under his breath, he muttered, "Shit."

"Okay, bone broth time," Kultrak declared, easing his wing and arm away as he began to rise. "Then your pain meds."

Groaning softly, Stanley admitted, "I know I need them, but I sure do hate how loopy they make me."

Pausing, Kultrak threaded his fingers through Stanley's hair, petting lightly. "It won't be for long."

Stanley huffed a breath, but even that hurt. "Yeah," he muttered begrudgingly, pushing lightly into the gentle caresses while realizing someone had removed his braid at some point.

Kultrak offered him a commiserating smile before dipping his head and pressing a quick, chaste kiss to the corner of Stanley's mouth. As the gargoyle sat up and swung one leg off the side of the bed, he was tempted to call Kultrak back and ask for a deeper kiss. Except, Stanley decided that would be sort of gross, considering he couldn't remember the last time he'd brushed.

I'm not even certain what day it is.

A second later, Kultrak came back with a thermos. He relaxed his back against a pillow, resting against the headboard. After screwing off the lid, he used it as a mug and filled it with a liquid that, to Stanley's surprise, still steamed, especially considering Kultrak had said it was from a couple of hours ago.

After placing the open canister on the nightstand, Kultrak considered Stanley. "I don't think you're ready to sit up yet." Then the gargoyle must have noticed something on the nightstand he'd missed for he chuckled and reached for it. "And your buddies must have thought of that."

Kultrak revealed a straw with a bendy end. He placed the tube into the cup and adjusted the end. Then he brought it close to Stanley's face.

Stanley took a deep whiff, and he groaned softly even as his stomach growled. He knew that smell. "Thai curry," he muttered. "My favorite."

"Yeah?"

Kultrak held the cup steady as Stanley wrapped his lips around the end of the straw and took a tentative sip. After finding the liquid hot, but not unbearably so, he took a deeper swallow. Stanley hummed and swallowed once more before using his tongue to push the straw from his mouth.

"Yeah," Stanley confirmed, licking his lips and savoring the flavor on his tongue. "Pauline makes it from scratch using the bone marrow of our cows right here on the ranch. It's damn fantastic."

"Huh." Before Stanley could lift his head and nab the straw again, Kultrak lifted the mug away. He brought it to his own lips and took a gulp. "Oh, that is tasty," Kultrak agreed, returning it to Stanley's lips.

When Stanley scowled at Kultrak, muttering *mine*, before wrapping his lips back around the straw, Kultrak chuckled, the sound deep and low.

"There's plenty more, my mate," Kultrak assured with a smirk. With his other hand, he skimmed his nails soothingly over Stanley's scalp. "And I'm sure Pauline has even more ready should I call for it."

Kultrak's touch sent a mixture of relaxation and arousal through Stanley. As he slowly sipped his drink, he did his best to ignore the way his prick was beginning to plump. Stanley knew he wouldn't be up to anything for . . . he wasn't certain how long.

With the meds that had been pumped into him, Stanley couldn't really remember the entirety of his diagnosis. As much as he wished he hadn't needed to go to the hospital, he knew it'd been the right call. Stanley had always avoided the medical industry unless absolutely necessary . . . which his boss and co-workers had assured him it was.

Stanley felt his eyes beginning to droop just as the sound of him hitting the dredges reached his ears.

"You want a refill, Stanley?" Kultrak asked softly, scraping his scalp gently to draw his attention.

Blinking open eyelids he didn't remember closing, Stanley murmured, "Don't think so." His brows furrowed as he asked curiously, "How'd you even know I hadn't fallen asleep with the straw in my mouth?"

Kultrak smiled at him, the expression appearing fond. "I was watching your Adam's apple." With a wink, he claimed, "Knew you were still taking a sip every few seconds or so."

Stanley nodded just a smidge. "Huh." After licking his lips, he admitted, "No refill. Gonna pass out soon."

"Then let's get that pill down you." Kultrak reached over, placing the cup on the nightstand. He never once stopped his gentle caresses to Stanley's scalp, which was starting to cause tingles to trickle down his chest. When Kultrak returned his attention to him, he pressed something to Stanley's bottom lip. "Open," he encouraged.

Acting on faith, Stanley did as he was ordered and accepted the pill on his tongue. He was planning to swallow it dry when Kultrak grabbed a bottle of water and touched it to his bottom lip. At the same time, the gargoyle stopped scratching his scalp and moved that hand to cradle his head, lifting gently.

Stanley took a sip of the water, then a second, and swallowed the pill. As Kultrak eased his head back to his pillow, Stanley felt it. His bladder twinged.

"Oh, shit," Stanley muttered, grimacing.

"What's wrong?" Kultrak swept his gaze over Stanley, obviously searching for the problem. He looked pensive. "Did I hurt you?"

"No. No, you didn't," Stanley quickly assured, even as he grimaced. "Um, I just, uh—"

"What, my mate?" The big gray gargoyle appeared so eager to please, which Stanley found oddly endearing. "What do you need? Your cell phone? Do you need to call your boss about something work-related?"

Stanley found that offer oddly tempting, but he knew there would be no point to it. It wasn't as if he could do anything. Nicholas would just ask Stanley how he was feeling before telling him to get plenty of rest and to let his mate take care of him.

Besides, that wasn't the issue.

Lifting a hand, Stanley gripped Kultrak's wrist before he could move away, perhaps to get said phone. "No, uh, actually—" Knowing he needed to bite the bullet, so to speak, Stanley admitted, "I need to piss."

Kultrak froze for one heartbeat, then two, before dipping his chin in a swift nod. "Okay." He swept his gaze over Stanley's sheet-covered form again. "Uh..." The gargoyle seemed to be at a loss for an instant. Then Kultrak shook himself out of ... whatever ... and asked, "What's the easiest way for us to do this, ya think?"

In truth, Stanley wasn't sure. He knew the second he tried to sit up, fiery agony would surge through his body. Having his side torn open by a horn just wasn't a good location for sitting . . . or walking . . . or any movement in general.

Yeah, Nicholas is right. I'm down for a few days.

Damn it.

Stanley blew out a breath as he met Kultrak's gaze. "I don't suppose you can help me stand up, could you?" When the gargoyle appeared conflicted, Stanley explained, "I know I need to do the best I can not to bend my torso, but I really gotta hit the head."

"What if I bring you a bottle to piss in?" Kultrak blurted even as he rose to his feet. Looking uncertain, he continued on a rush, "We can roll you to your good side, and I'll catch it for you or hold you steady as you do or—"

"Stop," Stanley ordered, holding up his hand. As much as it sucked and as embarrassing as it sounded, it was a decent idea. "That'll work."

"It will?" Kultrak sounded surprised.

Stanley didn't want to draw out the awkwardness. "Yeah. Uh, I have a bag of empty plastic bottles in my laundry room," he told the gargoyle. "Grab one for me, will ya?"

"Okay." Kultrak rushed from the room.

Listening to the gargoyle, Stanley could monitor his progress as he moved around the cabin. When the male opened the wrong door and closed it again, it occurred to him that he should have explained where the laundry room was. Stanley sighed and focused on breathing. At least the pill was taking effect, and the pain in his side was beginning to ebb a bit.

Of course, that also meant his mind was becoming a little fuzzy, too. Sleep was threatening, but he knew he couldn't give in. That would be a recipe for disaster . . . and a mess.

Ugh.

Stanley snapped open his eyes again just in time to watch

Kultrak return with an empty bottle. The gargoyle paused beside the bed, then gently pulled down the sheet. Doing his best to fight down a blush as his body was revealed—he hadn't even realized he was nude—Stanley began to try to roll to his left side, but instantly stopped when pain flashed through him.

"Just relax, my mate," Kultrak crooned, placing the bottle on the bed near his hip. "Let me help."

To Stanley's surprise, Kultrak also had a couple of hand towels with him. He placed them beside the bottle. Kultrak slid one arm under Stanley's shoulders while gripping his thigh with the other.

Carefully, Kultrak rolled Stanley partly onto his left side. He kept his arm under his shoulder to hold him steady while grabbing the towel with the other. Kultrak placed that under Stanley's thankfully flaccid dick—pain could do that to a man—and over his thigh and the bed, and Stanley instantly understood.

To catch the drips, just in case.

Then Kultrak grabbed the zero-calorie *Gatorade* bottle and brought the wide mouth toward Stanley's groin.

Yanking his brain out of his fuzziness—plus his surprise at Kultrak's thoughtfulness—Stanley grabbed the bottle. "I got this," he mumbled, fighting down his embarrassment.

Kultrak took him at his word and relinquished the plastic container.

Stanley positioned the head of his dick inside the opening, feeling himself lose the battle with his blush. Still, even with heat flooding his neck and cheeks, he didn't have any trouble releasing his bladder. Stanley even had to bite back a groan of pleasure as the pressure gave way.

A few minutes later, Kultrak took the half-filled bottle without a word, setting it on the floor. Then he used the second, damp cloth to wipe over Stanley's groin. After returning Stanley to his back, Kultrak pulled the sheet back over him.

"Be right back," Kultrak told him before leaving the room.

With a sigh, Stanley relaxed and allowed his eyelids to slide closed. He listened as Kultrak moved around his cabin. There was the sound of the toilet flushing, followed by the faucet.

Stanley had just begun to drift off when he felt the bed dip. Cracking an eyelid, he watched Kultrak ease down beside him. Then he returned his wing and arm to where they were before Stanley had woken, and he couldn't help but smile.

"Thank you, Kultrak," Stanley whispered, suddenly feeling damn grateful to have met the stoic, kind gargoyle.

"You're welcome, my mate." Kultrak pressed a light kiss to Stanley's temple before murmuring, "Get some rest."

Stanley obeyed, thinking that he sure could get used to having someone so attentive in his home and his bed.

CHAPTER SIX

After waking from roost, Kultrak immediately jumped to his feet. He wasted no time rushing to the door of the loft, throwing it open, and leaping out. Kultrak snapped out his wings and caught a current.

As Kultrak flew to his mate's cabin, from the corner of his eye, he noticed both Gurrando and Struano watching him. Both wore amused smiles. Relief filled Kultrak that neither of them thought he was shirking his duties by rushing to Stanley's side.

It had been two evenings since Stanley's accident, and Kultrak loved every second of hanging out with his mate, talking and learning about each other. Well, that was during the short stints that Stanley was awake, anyway. Kultrak was happy just to sit beside Stanley while he was sleeping, too.

The elders had moved some of the meetings to Stanley's front room. That way—while his mate was sleeping—they could include Kultrak.

Landing on the front porch, Kultrak reached for the door. He eased it open without knocking, just in case Stanley was sleeping. His nostrils were assailed with a myriad of scents, which was too bad.

Kultrak felt a little bad that Stanley's home no longer scented primarily of his mate, but he knew that those who were coming and going were offering his human support in his time of need.

Right then, Kultrak recognized Mitchel's scent. The human was mated to the gargoyle Sindrid, and he and Stanley shared a love of fantasy novels. Kultrak could hear Mitchel's soft tenor as he spoke of someone exploring an underground cavern.

Figuring that meant Stanley was awake, Kultrak headed to the bedroom. He stopped in the doorway and admired the sight of his mate lounging in bed. Stanley had been propped up on a couple of pillows—not sitting but not reclining entirely, either. Stanley had his head turned in Mitchel's direction. His eyelids were at half-mast, and a look of contentment creased his full lips.

The braid that Kultrak had left in Stanley's hair the morning before had mostly loosened, and he looked forward to removing the rest and brushing his mate's long black locks. For some reason, Kultrak found the action soothing. Plus, Stanley's scent of relaxation told him that his mate wasn't just placating him. His human enjoyed it just as much.

"Hey, Stanley," Kultrak greeted with a smile, moving slowly into the room. "You look good."

Stanley turned to focus on Kultrak, and the smile his mate blessed him with caused Kultrak's heart to skip a beat.

Gorgeous.

"Hi, Kultrak," Stanley replied, lifting his hand and beckoning. "We lost track of time."

"Good book?" Kultrak asked, glancing toward Mitchel—who'd stopped reading and was smiling at him—before refocusing on Stanley and taking his hand.

"Yep," Stanley responded, squeezing his hand while tugging on it. "Kiss." Waggling his brows, Stanley told him, "I brushed not too long ago."

Kultrak chuckled, pleased that Stanley was becoming comfortable with affection between them. "I would have kissed you regardless," he told him honestly, bending at the waist and using a hand on the mattress to support his weight.

Pressing his lips to Stanley's, Kultrak gently nibbled his bottom one. He lapped along it, and he hummed happily upon enjoying his human's flavor. When Stanley opened, Kultrak couldn't resist dipping his tongue in for a deeper taste, causing his arousal to flare.

A soft chuckle and the rustle of clothing drew Kultrak's attention, and he eased the kiss to an end. He spotted Mitchel rising to his feet, and after pecking one more kiss to Stanley's mouth, he straightened. Lifting a hand, Kultrak hoped to stall the human, who sported an amused expression.

"Please, do you mind staying a bit longer?" Kultrak urged, indicating the seat the man had just vacated. "I'm gonna shower, then get us a meal."

As much as Kultrak enjoyed kissing Stanley, he knew nothing could come of it. He needed a few minutes to take care of his aching cock. After that, he wanted to provide for his mate and share a conversation.

"Sure," Mitchel agreed readily enough. Pulling the book back out of the satchel he'd placed over his shoulder—a real live hardcover book—he added, "It'll give us time to finish this chapter."

Kultrak nodded his thanks before focusing on Stanley. "Guess I should have asked if that was okay with you," he admitted, seeing the smirk curving Stanley's firm lips. "Mind if I use your shower?" While Kultrak knew he could head to the bunkhouse or the main house to use the facilities, he rather liked the idea of sharing with his mate.

Stanley chuckled quietly, his dark eyes soft with amusement. "I don't mind." With a squeeze to Kultrak's hand, he ordered, "Be sure to come back and give me a kiss before heading to the kitchen. I'll call down there to see what they're offering that my stomach can handle."

While Stanley was no longer only on fluids, he still couldn't handle certain heavier foods.

Kultrak nodded. "Deal." After pressing a hard close-mouthed kiss to Stanley's mouth, he drew away. "Be back in a few."

Then Kultrak turned and exited the room. Even before he made it to the bathroom, he heard Mitchel begin reading once more. He slipped into the bathroom, closing the door behind him.

With a quiet groan, Kultrak yanked off his loincloth. The fabric wasn't much of a constraint to the erection throbbing at his groin, but it had still been uncomfortable. He moved to the shower and turned on the water, all the while eyeing the large jetted tub set up in the corner.

Can't wait until I can enjoy that with Stanley.

The idea of a wet naked Stanley lounging in the huge tub while Kultrak cradled him between his thighs, his erection nestled against his human's ass, caused his prick to jerk eagerly. With a groan, he stepped into the shower. Kultrak felt fortunate Stanley had indulged in his bathroom facilities, because it meant he barely had to tuck in his wings.

Grabbing the waterproof lube he'd found in there the prior day — *gods, I bet Stanley standing in here jacking off is a sight to behold* — Kultrak popped the cap. He squirted a generous portion into his palm. As Kultrak closed the lube and set it aside, he wrapped his slicked fingers around his jutting shaft.

Kultrak clenched his jaw, barely holding back his rumble of pleasure. Resting his free hand on the shower wall, he began jacking his hard length. He closed his eyes and bowed his head, bringing up the image of Stanley standing there doing the exact same thing in his mind.

While Kultrak had seen Stanley nude a number of times over the last couple of days while caring for him, the frail healing man in the bed wasn't the one he saw in his mind's eye.

Instead, Kultrak recalled the strong, vibrant human he'd first met. His skin had sported a healthy glow, and he'd stood tall and strong. That version of his mate leaned his back against the shower wall with his legs spread hips' distance apart. He had one hand gripping his length, jacking his flushed cock steadily, as he rolled his heavy testicles with the other. His head was tipped back, his lips were parted, and pleasure flushed his cheeks to a rosy hue.

Kultrak couldn't hold back his groan as he enjoyed the provocative image. The water would run down Stanley's chest in thick rivulets, accentuating his muscular chest and delineated abdominals. His human would rock his lean hips, fucking his fist in short, sharp jabs. His breath would come in soft gasps as he chased his orgasm.

Just as Kultrak imagined the look of ecstasy that would cross Stanley's face as he came—the glorious arc of his white seed as he erupted like a fountain—he felt his own orgasm slam through him. His balls pulled tight as his erection swelled and pulsed. Barking a cry, Kultrak felt his body shake with the force of his release, his knees trembling, and he needed to lock them to keep standing.

Resting his head on the tile wall next to his hand, Kultrak panted harshly as he slowed the hand on his prick. He continued to tug slowly, drawing out a couple extra spurts and extending his pleasure. Swallowing hard, he stared at the thick stream of seed as it dripped down the wall to mix with the water and disappear down the drain.

Kultrak desperately wanted to spray his seed somewhere else—namely, in Stanley's ass. Just the thought of coating his mate's inner walls caused his prick to twitch, and renewed heat flowed south. He groaned for a new reason, shaking his head.

Grabbing the body wash and loofah—he liked that Stanley enjoyed such things—Kultrak got down to the business of scrubbing himself. He hoped the sound of the water had muffled his noises so the other men in the house hadn't heard. Kultrak would never want to put any pressure on Stanley, even if he hadn't been healing.

Once clean, Kultrak shut off the water, opened the door, and grabbed a towel. He rubbed it over his chest, then down his legs. After stepping onto the plush bath mat, he wrapped it around his waist. Next, Kultrak grabbed a towel and twisted it around his hair.

Kultrak opened the linen closet and smiled. Pulling out a clean loincloth, he reveled in the fact that Stanley had been the one to suggest that he place some there. His mate was opening his home to him, and Kultrak had every intention of never leaving.

Well, not until we need to change his identity and are forced to leave the area.

Realizing he still had to talk to Stanley about that, Kultrak dropped the towel and replaced it with the loincloth. He picked up the towel and used it to wipe himself down some more. Once his hide was dry, he opened the door that joined the bathroom with the bedroom's walk-in closet and tossed it into the laundry basket. Kultrak towel-dried his hair as best he could, then did the same with the second one.

Kultrak slipped through the closet's other door, opening to the bedroom. Pausing, he stared at the sight before him. Stanley was sitting up a little bit more in the bed, and there was a checkered blanket spread out along the foot of it.

On the checkered blanket was an impressive spread of breakfast foods. There were premade burritos, sausage sandwiches on English muffins, a container of biscuits and gravy, scrambled eggs with peppers and cheese in them, toast, and hash browns. The aroma filling the room caused Kultrak's stomach to growl and his mouth to water.

"Wow," Kultrak rumbled, easing closer. "This is . . . impressive."

Stanley relaxed on the bed, eyeing him with a smile. "I really did lose track of time. I'd hoped to have this ready for us when you first arrived," he admitted, lifting one shoulder in a half-shrug. Then Stanley smirked as he waggled his brows.

"But your extra-long shower did the trick. Have fun in there?"

Kultrak felt a bit of blood flood his cheeks, and he groaned, lowering his gaze. "Shit. Did you hear me?" Peering at Stanley, worry filling him, he told him, "I'd never want to make you feel like you should, uh, or that you're not taking care of my needs. This isn't—"

"Stop, Kultrak," Stanley ordered, waving his hand as if shooing away a fly. "Just stop. I don't feel like that at all." Patting the bed, Stanley urged, "Come here and have a meal with me. We'll talk about that."

A mixture of relief and trepidation filled Kultrak, but he did as his mate bid. He eased onto what he considered *his side* of the bed. He noticed a pale orange drink with bubbles sitting on his nightstand.

Stanley must have caught him eyeing it, for his human simply stated, "Mimosa."

Kultrak snapped his attention to Stanley's nightstand and spotted a similar drink on the foreman's side of the bed.

Scoffing softly, Stanley obviously read Kultrak's silent question. "Mine is a light orange drink." He winked. "No alcohol."

Twisting his lips into a wry smile, Kultrak met Stanley's gaze. "Sorry. I know you're a grown man, but—"

"You're a gargoyle, a paranormal, and I'm your mate." Stanley's expression appeared understanding. "I do understand. Really." His attention drifted to the right, toward the main house far beyond the cabin's walls. "I've watched a lot of pairs come together over the last few years." Stanley returned his attention to Kultrak. "Even still, I never expected it to happen to me, so it came as a shock."

Nodding slowly, Kultrak tried to understand where Stanley was headed with their meal. His words sounded cautionary, even as the spread gave it a date-like feel. Kultrak wasn't certain how to respond to Stanley's statement.

"So, anyway, dig in," Stanley encouraged, indicating the food. "I'm hoping you'll fix me a plate." He pointed at the pair of plates near the foot of the bed. "I don't plan to have too much, but I'm looking forward to trying a couple bites of everything."

Kultrak was happy to have something to do. Easing forward, he grabbed the top plate. "What can I get you?"

Stanley smirked as if not surprised that Kultrak planned to feed him first. "I'd love a sausage, egg, and cheese muffin sandwich," he told him, pointing. "And if you could put two pieces of toast on the plate and then pile a bunch of scrambled eggs on top, that'll be good for me." As an afterthought, Stanley added, "Oh, and a scoop of the hash browns. There's ketchup in that tub."

Nodding, Kultrak did as he'd been instructed, whipping up Stanley's plate. He opened the indicated container and found it full of ketchup packets. After placing half a dozen of them on Stanley's plate, he handed it to his mate along with silverware.

"Thanks," Stanley murmured, holding the plate against his left pectoral. He skipped the fork in favor of picking up the egg-covered toast and bringing it to his mouth.

While Kultrak fixed his own plate, taking a healthy portion of everything and knowing he would be going back for seconds and maybe thirds, he watched in silence as Stanley crunched his way through his eggs and toast.

Kultrak grabbed ketchup for himself and realized a number of picante sauce packets were in there, too, so he took some for his burrito. He relaxed back again, content to eat in silence for a moment, happy in the knowledge that his mate was beside him.

"So, I'm just going to lay this out there," Stanley stated slowly, picking up a ketchup packet. He paused to use his teeth to open it. As he squirted the condiment onto his hash browns, Stanley eyed Kultrak. "When I'm well enough, I'd like to bond with you."

Kultrak nearly choked on the bite of muffin sandwich he'd just taken, his mate's unexpected comment completely throwing him for a loop.

Did I really hear what I thought I heard?

CHAPTER SEVEN

Seeing Kultrak cough around the mouthful of sandwich he'd just taken, Stanley realized he should have eased into his announcement a little bit. The gargoyle stared at him in wide-eyed shock. His deep gray eyes stared at Stanley intensely, as if he couldn't believe what he'd just heard.

I could plumb knock him over with a feather, or so the saying goes.

Stanley moved his plate to his thigh to free up his left hand. Reaching over, he gripped Kultrak's forearm. He rubbed his thumb over the man's thick hide, enjoying the feel of the unique skin.

"I guess I should have approached that a little differently," Stanley admitted, smiling at Kultrak with amusement. "But I thought after all our talks that somehow you'd know but was just waiting for verbal confirmation." Realizing how silly that sounded, Stanley scoffed. "Guess we'll have to work on our mind-reading techniques, huh?"

"That's, uh—" Kultrak paused to clear his throat. His smile appeared a little concerned. "That's a vampire thing." With furrowed brow ridges, Kultrak reminded him, "Gargoyles don't form a mind-link. We're the ones who can impregnate our male mates."

Kultrak blurted out that last bit as if he were worried it would be a deal-breaker.

As if I don't know.

"I was just teasing, Kultrak," Stanley told him with a smile, squeezing his forearm once more before releasing him so he could return to his meal. "And as far as the knocking up your male mate thing, I'm aware." Unable to help himself, Stanley's tone turned a little wistful. "And I'm not averse to carrying your young. I was an only child, and I always wondered what it would be like to have siblings, so we'd need to have at least two. Just not right now. I've only caught bits and pieces of why you guys actually came here," Stanley admitted, feeling a little frustrated. "I think everyone is worried about causing me alarm or something while recovering, but all they're really doing is stressing me out, so, uh, we'll talk about having kids after whatever is dealt with. Plus, I'd really prefer to have them here at the ranch. This is a great place to grow up, and—" Realizing he was rambling, Stanley shoved a bite of eggs and toast in his mouth to get himself to shut up.

"Y-You want kids?" Kultrak seemed absolutely flabbergasted by that. "Even though it's *you* who'll have to carry them?"

Ah, so that's what he's hung up on.

Stanley smiled around his bite of food as he nodded once.

"I-I admit, I wasn't expecting that," Kultrak rumbled, clearly surprised. Although a smile was beginning to tip up the corners of his lips. "Most humans have to take a year or more to wrap their heads around that." Kultrak grinned at him. "And, yeah, I want kids."

After swallowing another bite of food, Stanley chuckled as he smiled at Kultrak. "Well, I've been living with the knowledge for years already," he reminded his gargoyle. *I like that thought. My gargoyle.* "Not to mention, Shaw is already carrying. He's due in a month." Kultrak seemed to be having a hard time finding his tongue, so Stanley continued, "There's cinnamon rolls in that tray." He pointed at one Kultrak hadn't seemed to notice. "We should definitely eat some." A thought occurred to Stanley, and it was his turn to feel worried. "You aren't one of those gargoyles that's immune to cinnamon, are you?"

Stanley's question finally seemed to yank Kultrak out of his shock, and he barked a laugh. "No, I'm not immune to cinnamon," he assured. Wrinkling his nose, he muttered, "Glad of it, too. I always thought those potions we used to have to get from witches were nasty."

Snorting, Stanley nodded. "I've seen Ssimeas holding his nose while drinking them a time or two." Seeing Kultrak's arched eyebrow ridge, he answered the gargoyle's silent question. "He's immune to cinnamon, and Attain is allergic, so Maggie makes Ssimeas the potion. I hear she's trying to figure out a way to make them more palatable, but since she's so late in her pregnancy, she hasn't been able to focus on it much."

"Understandable," Kultrak murmured. He fell silent for a moment, his gaze sweeping over Stanley several times. "I-I'd hoped you'd want to bond with me soon," he rumbled, hope filling his tone. "We just hadn't said anything about it the last couple of days."

Stanley blew out a breath, even as he smiled. "Yeah. We've kept things light, generic stuff about each other." Then he rolled his eyes and grumbled, "Plus, I do more sleeping than not, and it's not like summer daylight hours gives you a lot of time out of roost."

Kultrak dipped his chin in acknowledgment of that fact. "Well, I'm . . ." He paused and shook his head. He scoffed. Meeting Stanley's gaze, Kultrak told him with deep affection in his tone, "I can't even express how pleased I am, how much I'm looking forward to it, how much I want to spend the rest of my many years building a life with you."

Humming around his last bite of toast and eggs — Stanley appreciated how easy it was to eat with one hand — he nodded with a smirk. "Guess that's something we never covered. How old are you?" he asked curiously.

"Just shy of eight centuries," Kultrak revealed, looking

worried. He placed a hand on Stanley's elbow and lightly teased the skin there. "I know it seems like a long time. It's why we value our mates so highly."

After wiping his fingers on a napkin, Stanley placed his hand over Kultrak's and squeezed reassuringly. "I know." He felt the undeniable need to reassure his gargoyle, but he could feel the need for sleep beginning to pull at him. "God, I hate feeling so weak," he grumbled. Blinking quickly, Stanley noticed Kultrak's look of concern, and he immediately told him, "But I'm healing. Just another two days of these meds that kick my ass, then I'm going to wean off the stronger shit."

"Are you sure?" Kultrak looked concerned. "I don't want you in pain."

Stanley scoffed. "Yeah, I'm sure. I don't want to be so out of it." With a grin and an eyebrow waggle, he told his gargoyle, "I have a life to build with my gargoyle." Upon seeing the way Kultrak's gray eyes darkened to a stormy color, betraying his pleasure upon hearing Stanley's words, he suddenly felt like a heel for worrying the male. "I'm sorry you ever doubted us, Kultrak," Stanley told him, feeling compelled to apologize. "I know I didn't respond the best at first, but . . . I just . . . didn't understand, I guess."

"Understand what?" Kultrak asked curiously.

"Well." Stanley paused, thinking on how to explain. "I've seen other humans react to the pull and just jump in after a day or two, and I just . . . I didn't understand it." He frowned at his nearly empty plate, sorting his thoughts. "I've tried relationships in the past. Once with a woman and once with a man." When Stanley heard Kultrak growl softly, he snapped his attention to the male. "I know paranormals are possessive and don't like hearing about our pasts, but please, just hear me out a sec."

Stanley could see a tick flex in Kultrak's jaw, but the gargoyle nodded. He reached over and moved Stanley's plate back to his thighs so he could take his left hand. Meeting Stanley's gaze, Kultrak nodded once as if to tell him that he was ready for Stanley to continue.

After offering Kultrak a reassuring squeeze to his hand, Stanley told him, "In the spirit of keeping it brief, I never lived with them, but I did think we were exclusive." Waving his right hand, Stanley absently indicated the ranch. "I was already working here, under my father, Richard, who was the foreman at the time. He was training me in all aspects of the ranch, probably already planning for me to take over for him, so my free time really was limited. All that I had, though, I used to go see my special someone." Scoffing, Stanley shook his head. "Let's just say, I popped in on my lady, wanting to surprise her with a romantic evening meal, and found her in bed with another man."

Kultrak growled, his hand tightening on Stanley's, but he didn't say anything.

Plowing ahead, Stanley explained, "I'm bisexual, so I figured I'd try a man, instead." He rolled his eyes. "As far as I know, the man was faithful, but he got tired of the ranch always coming first. He moved to the city, saying he was tired of never being a priority and that he wanted to find someone who could actually appreciate him."

Stanley could still hear those accusations ringing in his ears, and he'd taken them to heart. "He was right. The ranch did always come first." With a soft scoff, he mumbled, "He did deserve better than what I could give him. Then my father wanted to retire, I took over as foreman, and with the increased workload, I never looked for another." With a shrug, Stanley admitted, "I convinced myself that one-night stands were enough for me, and I've lived that way for over eleven years."

Turning his head, Stanley held Kultrak's gaze as he told

him, "Until you came along and cared for me with no expectations except me allowing you to be around, I'd forgotten how lonely my life was." He squeezed Kultrak's thick fingers while smiling at him. "Thank you."

"I'd do anything for you, my mate," Kultrak rumbled, bringing Stanley's hand to his lips. He pressed a soft kiss to Stanley's palm while holding his gaze. "And I'll never leave you or cheat on you."

Stanley felt tingles work up his arm, starting from the point of Kultrak's surprisingly soft lips. The hairs on his arm stood on end. He even felt his nipples bead.

Damn. Such a small contact with such a big response.

"I know that, too." Stanley hesitated, but he knew he needed to ask about one more thing. "Uh, I guess another big thing is, um, how long do you think you're going to be here at the ranch? I know this isn't your home."

Great Spirits, am I really ready to give up everything for this gargoyle?

Stanley honestly wasn't certain.

To Stanley's surprise, Kultrak grinned widely. "This will be our home for the foreseeable future. That's something I wanted to talk to you about."

"Really?" Stanley couldn't help his surprise. Jumping to a conclusion, he asked, "Does this have something to do with what's going on with the elder?"

"Exactly," Kultrak confirmed. Blowing out a breath, he admitted, "We believe one of our elders has gone rogue and has even killed another elder. Something to do with gargoyle superiority and supremacy due to our strength and longevity." A low growl escaped Kultrak as he continued, "We're in the process of confirming if any other elders are involved. Once we confirm who's innocent, we're encouraging them to move here, using the ranch as a safe hub to plan and figure out Elder Laagstine's plan and associates."

"Elder Laagstine?" Stanley repeated. Then he realized

what he did and shook his head, squeezing Kultrak's hand when he opened his mouth as if to continue explaining. "Okay, that's not the important bit." Stanley knew his brain was slowing down with his rising fatigue, and he needed to confirm something else before he allowed sleep to claim him once more. "So, you're staying here for however long it takes to figure out this elder conspiracy?"

"Not exactly," Kultrak replied, and a stab of disappointment hit Stanley. That feeling was replaced with pleasure when Kultrak continued, "I'm staying here with you until either we're forced to move due to human culture catching on that we don't age, or until you're ready to move somewhere else."

"Really?" It was Stanley's turn to feel shock. "Just like that?"

Kultrak nodded. "Just like that." Releasing Stanley's hand while setting his plate aside, he eased closer to him. Kultrak threaded his fingers through Stanley's hair, scratching lightly along his scalp in that way he was coming to love. "This is your home. You said you want to raise our hatchlings here. And over the last couple of days, I've seen how your family has pulled together to care for not just you, but everyone here."

"My family?" Stanley couldn't help but question that. "It's just my father and me. I never knew my mother."

Scoffing, Kultrak shook his head. His gray eyes twinkled. "You have family," the gargoyle declared. "A whole house full of them." Kultrak glanced in the direction of the main house before refocusing on Stanley with a grin. "Just because they're not blood doesn't mean they're not your family."

Stanley chuckled softly as he processed that. "Huh. Guess you're right," he murmured. When Kultrak scraped his claws lightly down his scalp to the nape of his neck to massage there gently, Stanley lost his train of thought as heat warmed his chest and tingles worked down his spine. "Hmmmm."

"Now that we have those few things cleared up," Kultrak rumbled, leaning closer. "I think it's time you stop fighting the pull of sleep." Tipping toward him, Kultrak pressed a kiss to Stanley's temple before murmuring into his ear, "Can I help you relax so you can rest comfortably?"

As if to make certain Stanley didn't miss his meaning, Kultrak rested his free hand on his left shoulder. He slid it down his pectoral, stopping a second to flick Stanley's peaked nipple, drawing a hiss from him. Kultrak continued to slide his hand farther down under the blanket to tease his nails along Stanley's good side.

Stanley felt his breathing hitch. Heat flooded his groin, and his prick thickened. Considering he always seemed to be in a state of semi-arousal around Kultrak, even with the pain of the stitches in his side and his healing skin, it didn't take long for his cock to thicken to full mast, tenting the sheet.

"May I?" Kultrak pressed, and Stanley realized he'd been too busy enjoying the gargoyle's touch to respond.

After swallowing hard, getting a little moisture into his throat, Stanley whispered, "Oh, Great Spirits, yes." A tremble of anticipation worked through him. He gripped Kultrak's wrist and pushed, trying to urge him lower. "Want that so much."

The pressure of Stanley flexing his arm muscles caused his stomach to clench, and a flash of pain to his side drew a hiss from him.

"Just relax, Stanley," Kultrak urged, ignoring his desire and pulling his hand away. "I'll take care of everything."

Stanley groaned when Kultrak moved farther away, but then the gargoyle helped him sit up a little and removed the extra pillows Mitchel had placed behind him so he was sort of sitting up. Once Stanley was lying flat again, Kultrak slipped into bed beside him. His gargoyle levered over him, his thick white hair falling like a curtain around them.

"Just relax and enjoy, my mate. I'll take care of everything," Kultrak crooned, sliding his right hand back into Stanley's hair. The gargoyle seemed to know exactly what massaging his claws through Stanley's hair did to him, and Kultrak started teasing along his flesh. "Try not to flex too much. I don't want you hurt from this."

Nodding just enough to offer confirmation without pulling away from Kultrak's amazing ministration, Stanley agreed as he did his best to relax.

"There you go," Kultrak purred. "That's the way."

Kultrak didn't wait for a response. In that instant, he slipped his hand back under the sheet. Without any shyness, as if he had every right to touch, Kultrak wrapped his large warm hand around Stanley's erection and began to jack him.

Stanley groaned and shivered, doing his best to stay relaxed as Kultrak began a slow, steady pace. The gargoyle's calloused fingers created the most delicious friction on Stanley's engorged organ. Fissures of delicious tingles coursed straight to his groin.

As much as Stanley wanted to plant his feet and buck up into Kultrak's hold, he resisted. He knew that wouldn't help, no matter what his instincts told him. Instead, Stanley gripped the forearm of the arm Kultrak used to massage his scalp, needing something to keep himself grounded.

Kultrak nuzzled his cheek against Stanley's. "Give in," he urged huskily. "Give in to the pleasure your mate gives you."

Then Kultrak began to trill.

Stanley barked a cry as the vibrations transferred straight to his head and his cock and everywhere else Kultrak's body touched him. Unable to resist, his balls pulled tight. His cock jerked and twitched in Kultrak's grip as his orgasm bowled through his system.

Pulse after pulse of seed surged from his cock, sending

heady waves of bliss thrumming through Stanley's body. He groaned Kultrak's name as his senses soared. Spots danced across his vision as he floated blissfully on endorphins.

Stanley thought Kultrak rumbled, "Gorgeous," before he drifted into a relaxing sleep.

CHAPTER EIGHT

K ultrak ignored the renewed ache in his groin as he admired Stanley's relaxed features. His naturally bronzed cheeks continued to glow from his release, even as he drifted into sleep. The smile of pleasure that graced his lips tempted Kultrak to kiss him.

Not wanting to reawaken Stanley, Kultrak resisted.

Instead, Kultrak eased off the bed. He hurried to the bathroom and wetted down a cloth. Upon returning to the bedroom, Kultrak made quick work of cleaning up his lover.

Finally, Stanley is my lover.

As Kultrak picked up the remaining food and carried it all into the front room, he marveled at how things could change in just a few minutes. His mate had told him that he accepted him, that he wanted to bond with him, and that he even wanted to carry his young. Kultrak couldn't help but strut a little, feeling ten feet tall.

Even though it couldn't happen right away, that didn't change Kultrak's excitement. They could exchange mating bites and blood, and that would start the bonding process. If Kultrak believed the stories, it would also help jumpstart Stanley's healing.

The sooner Stanley is healed, the sooner we can complete our bond.

Just thinking of bonding with Stanley caused Kultrak's prick to twitch behind his loincloth. He could hardly wait. After clearing the extra food and drink from the bedroom, Kultrak opened the container that Stanley had told him contained the cinnamon rolls. Even as he imagined Stanley swollen with his egg, Kultrak ate a cinnamon roll in three bites.

He would respect Stanley's wish to get the elder problem sorted first.

Still need to explain everything about that.

Returning to the bedroom, Kultrak leaned on the door-frame and took a moment to admire his mate in the bed. He smiled, sighing contentedly. Kultrak loved that he'd put that expression on Stanley's face and intended to do it as often as possible.

The chime of his phone caught Kultrak's attention, and he turned away from the provocative sight. Locating his phone on the nightstand, he hit the button to accept the call from Gurrando. Kultrak lifted his phone to his ear as he quietly exited the room.

Gurrando didn't wait for him to say anything. "I'm sorry to interrupt, Kultrak," he stated softly, probably guessing that Stanley might be asleep. "Bodb is sending Lludd to sit with Stanley," he told him, referring to Bodb's youngest brother. The gargoyle was mated to the town sheriff. "I need you here."

"Yes, sir," Kultrak replied softly, leaving Stanley's door open a crack. "Stanley just fell asleep."

"Okay. I'll tell Lludd to bring a book," Gurrando stated with amusement. "See you soon."

Kultrak bit back a snort as his elder disconnected the call. He knew that Lludd wasn't much of a reader. Instead, the big enforcer had fallen in love with video games on his cell phone. Evidently, Arthur had turned Lludd onto them.

Heading to the front window, Kultrak peered out the glass while listening for Stanley, just in case his mate woke in the next few minutes. He didn't. A couple of moments later, Kultrak spotted Lludd striding across the clearing, his dark wings billowing behind him.

Meeting the other male on the porch, Kultrak greeted him

with a head nod. "Thank you for sitting with Stanley."

Lludd offered an amused smirk. "I'm the one getting a break." Patting Kultrak's upper arm, he told him, "If anything happens, I'll text you."

Kultrak barely resisted arching a brow in question. If Lludd had been ordered to text him as opposed to calling him, it meant whatever was going on, they couldn't be disturbed. That meant it was serious elder business.

Kultrak wondered what had happened since he'd risen from roost and left Gurrando's side. "Thank you," he replied simply before hustling to the main house. He spotted Biscane just inside the door, and the other gargoyle beckoned for him to follow. After falling into step flanking the male, Kultrak quietly asked, "Can you tell me what's going on?"

"Elder Cliatno is arriving soon," Biscane revealed.

Lifting his brow ridges, surprise filling him, Kultrak muttered, "Has he been cleared?"

"No," Biscane answered shortly, which explained why Gurrando wanted Kultrak there.

Gurrando didn't know if Cliatno could be trusted, and he wanted both his enforcers to watch his back.

"What enforcers are going to be with Cliatno?" Kultrak asked, hoping to get a feel for the strength of the incoming party.

"I haven't heard," Biscane replied. "Nor a confirmed number."

Kultrak hummed, not liking that response one bit. Normally, sharing that information was for courtesy. After all, if a gargoyle entered another's territory with a large force, it could be taken as an act of aggression.

Biscane led the way into the large study where they'd met the first night.

After stepping inside and taking a quick scan of the room, Kultrak strode to Gurrando's side. His elder dipped his chin in a nod of greeting, but he didn't speak. Struano offered him a slight smile before returning his attention to Bodb, who stood conferring with a vampire—Spieron, if he remembered correctly.

A moment later, Bodb nodded, and Spieron left the room. He turned to face everyone, announcing, "We still haven't received confirmation from Cliatno as to the number of his enforcers, and now he's not answering his phone." Roving his gaze over the room, Bodb ordered, "I'd like my people spread out in pairs. Stay alert." Turning his attention to Nicholas, he stated, "It may be best for you to encourage Sandra to take Maggie into the safe room. Virgil and Shaw, too."

"I'll mention it to them," Nicholas replied, crossing his arms over his chest. "But if you think I'm going to stay down there with them, you have another thing coming."

Bodb smiled ruefully at Nicholas. "If I thought you would stay, I would have mentioned it." Then he grimaced. "But if Cliatno is on the up and up, then your absence could be taken as a slight."

"Politics," Nicholas grumbled, shaking his head.

Nodding, Bodb muttered, "Politics."

Considering they were sending their pregnant members to a safe room, Kultrak couldn't help but cut in, "Should I move Stanley there, too?" In truth, Kultrak hadn't even realized there was a safe room on the property.

"He won't thank you if you do that without permission," Nicholas told him with a smirk. "And I heard he was asleep." Sobering, he added, "He's an unclaimed human, and no one outside of us knows that he's your mate. He won't be on their radar if there really is a problem, and we're not just being paranoid."

"I'll join Lludd," Biscane declared. "My mate is working at his condo in town tonight, so no way they'll be able to target him."

Kultrak murmured his thanks, knowing Biscane's mate, Jory, was a lawyer who still spent most of his time in town. From what he understood, Biscane had switched to working mostly days. Thinking about it, Kultrak realized that Lludd's sheriff mate must be pulling a night shift, too.

The group of gargoyles that worked as Bodb's enforcers worked hard to accommodate everyone and their mates' schedules, affording pairs with plenty of time together.

And Stanley didn't think he had a family.

"Everyone already knows their assignments," Bodb declared, sweeping his gaze over everyone. "If anything looks out of place, report it." His dark eyes narrowed as he ordered, "No one plays the hero. We're a team here, and we work together."

After getting murmurs of acknowledgment from everyone, they all began to drift from the room to do whatever their pre-arranged orders were.

Kultrak had to admit to himself that he was impressed with the group's organization. Once everyone filed out, he murmured to Gurrando, "So, uh, what do we do?"

"Stand around and wait," Gurrando replied, only sounding a tiny bit disgruntled. He crossed his arms over his chest and sighed as he smirked at Kultrak. "Drawbacks of becoming an elder. I don't go out looking for trouble. I have to wait until it comes to me."

Scoffing, Kultrak nodded. Worry filled him as his thoughts turned to Stanley. His mate was asleep, injured, and vulnerable, and not even in the same house as him. Kultrak knew he needed to have faith in Lludd and Biscane, but it was difficult.

"Tell me some good news," Gurrando urged, crossing to the sideboard. "How's Stanley? Is he feeling better?" He reached into the mini-fridge below it and pulled out a bottle of cranberry juice. "Want anything?"

"I'll take a lemonade," Struano requested, moving toward the elder.

"An iced tea, if they have it," Kultrak replied, following his fellow gargoyles' leads, trying to relax. As soon as he'd taken the bottle, he grinned at Gurrando. "And Stanley's doing well. In fact, he prepared a meal for me, and . . . he wants to bond as soon as he's well enough."

Struano swallowed his lemonade with a gulp before he grinned widely, showing off his pointed teeth. "That's fantastic, Kultrak." Slapping him on the shoulder, Struano asked, "Is it okay to ask what changed his mind?" He waggled his brows. "Or are you just that persuasive?"

Kultrak scoffed as he rolled his eyes at the other enforcer's antics. "No, I wouldn't use sex to coerce him." Although, the idea had definitely crossed Kultrak's mind.

"Is it because you told him we're sticking around for the foreseeable future?" Gurrando guessed.

"No, not that either," Kultrak admitted. With a shrug, he told his friends, "He told me right as we started eating. I just about choked on the bite of sandwich I'd taken." Lifting a hand to stall their questions, Kultrak thought about the best way to answer. Finally, he decided on, "He had to work through some personal issues, and, as odd as it sounds, needing to care for him without the stress of bonding right away ended up being the best thing."

"Huh." Struano didn't look like he understood, and Kultrak didn't have any desire to try to explain it further to him.

Gurrando patted Kultrak on his shoulder. "Well, I'm damn happy for you, my friend."

"Thank you." Kultrak couldn't stop smiling. "I can hardly wait."

"Gladstone just reported spotting five coming in fast," Spieron announced, entering the room with vampire speed.

Just that fast, Kultrak's smile faded.

"Attacking?" Bodb demanded.

Spieron shook his head. "Two are helping a third stay in

the air, and two are acting as rearguards." His eyes narrowed, and a growl rumbled from him as he listened to whoever was speaking in his earpiece. "There are six coming up behind them, fast and hard."

"Can Gladstone confirm the identity of any of them?" Bodb asked, moving toward the door that led to a hall close to the back deck.

"Just received word from Claude," Spieron told them, his eyes widening. "One of the two helping the injured gargoyle is Elder Cliatno."

"Then we help," Bodb stated, leading the way out of the room. "Tell Gladstone, Lebone, and Claude to engage if any of the six following make a move to attack the rearguard or to flank them."

"Yes, sir," Spieron replied immediately before issuing orders through his headpiece.

"Who's Claude again?" Kultrak asked, trying to put a face to the name.

"Human sniper on the roof," Struano murmured, answering. "He's mated to the other vampire here, Darian."

"Ah, yes." Kultrak nodded, recalling reading the report that stated Claude had been on the wrong side of paranormals at one point, and his mind had been tampered with by a demon. It had essentially left him with an odd sort of paranormal PTSD, and the people here were helping him get a handle on it.

When they walked outside, Kultrak heard the crack of a high-powered rifle echo through the air. As much as he wanted to fly toward the forms he could just make out in the distance, he knew his place was at his elder's side.

CHAPTER NINE

The unmistakable crack of a rifle jerked Stanley out of one of the best sleeps he could ever remember. Frowning, he glanced around for Kultrak, but he didn't see him. Stanley listened intently, wondering not only where his gargoyle was but what the hell was going on.

Why would someone be shooting at night?

The ranch occasionally had a problem with coyotes or a cougar sniffing around the herd during spring calving season, but there'd never been anything close to the ranch houses.

Stanley made out the low rumble of a pair of male voices coming from his front room, but neither of them was Kultrak. He listened more intently and realized with surprise that they were Biscane and Lludd. That was odd.

Just as Stanley prepared to call out, he heard a thud on the roof of his cabin, followed by the crack of the rifle again.

What the hell is going on?

One of the gargoyles in his cabin snarled, and the other hissed. "We stay here," Lludd stated. Although he didn't sound happy about it.

"How the hell did they get so close?" Biscane asked the question, but he didn't really sound as if he expected Lludd to answer it. "And how many are there?"

Lludd just grunted in response.

Stanley briefly wondered if whatever was happening had anything to do with that rogue elder Kultrak had mentioned. While he knew it hadn't been the right time, he still wished he had more information. Stanley opened his mouth to call out to the others when the sound of breaking glass filled the air. A second later, roars, hisses, thuds, and snarls sounded way too close.

Son of a bitch!

Gritting his teeth, Stanley forced his body to move. He fought against the spots threatening his vision as he eased his legs over the side of the bed. Stanley levered to his feet, breathing through the fiery stabs of agony working along his side.

Stanley listened to the commotion continuing in his front room as he limped slowly to the closet, using the nightstand and wall as support. Using the low light from the nightstand — the guys had all gotten used to leaving it on the lowest setting, even when he slept — he peered behind the door. His twenty-two was there, right where he'd left it.

Grabbing the small-caliber rifle, Stanley barely stifled his cry of pain. He quickly checked how many bullets he had in the weapon before cocking it and moving the rifle to his left hand. After tucking his right arm around his side, Stanley breathed deeply and pushed past the pain.

While Stanley wasn't much of a shot while shooting from the hip with his left hand, he didn't think he would need to be. If a gargoyle or other paranormal that he didn't know was coming at him, he intended to wait until point-blank range to fire. That would give him the optimal chance for the twenty-two to do enough damage to slow or stop it.

Crossing to the other side of his closet, Stanley locked the door that led to the bathroom. He returned to the doorway of the bedroom closet. By then, he felt his legs trembling as spots danced across his vision. Sweat slicked his skin and dripped down his temple, making his hair stick to his face, but he didn't have the energy to push it away.

Stanley leaned his left shoulder against the doorframe and waited. Concentrating on the noises coming from the main room, he tried to figure out who could be attacking, but no one was talking—not even Lludd or Biscane. Instead, the noises consisted of thuds, roars, curses, and snarls.

For a few seconds, the noises seemed to quiet, and Stanley hoped whatever it was was over.

In the next instant, a gargoyle's huge frame slammed into the slightly open door and came sailing into the room.

Stanley stared at the pale-brown gargoyle, thinking at first that it was Gladstone. Except, when it rose, he didn't recognize the features, and the sneer curling the paranormal's lips caused Stanley's heart to race. When the gargoyle pinned his brown-eyed gaze upon him, Stanley spotted the hatred within their depths.

"Human," the gargoyle sneered, disdain dripping from that one word.

"Get out of my house," Stanley ordered, leveling his rifle on the beast. "Now."

Curling his full lips, the gargoyle spread his wings and leaped on the bed—the only furniture between them. "Useless human." He lifted his arms, his black claws at the ready, clearly stalking Stanley.

When the gargoyle leaped, Stanley lifted the barrel a little higher and pulled the trigger. The bullet hit the gargoyle's torso, knocking him back a bit. The gargoyle roared and quickly used his wings to catch himself. Flying in the middle of Stanley's bedroom, the beast looked down at his chest, taking in the blood oozing from the small hole in his chest.

Stanley took those precious few seconds to awkwardly shuck the twenty-two shell casing and reload. He managed to raise his gun up just in time to fire again, aiming a little bit higher. The slug found a home in the gargoyle's upper chest, but the paranormal recovered quicker that time.

Fortunately, with the adrenaline raging through his veins, Stanley found it easier to fight through the pain. He switched the weapon to his dominant hand, reloading at the same time.

Bringing the rifle to his shoulder, Stanley aimed and fired once more.

The gargoyle's head snapped back, and he collapsed onto Stanley's bed.

Not taking any chances, Stanley reloaded again. He carefully eased forward, rounding the bed as he took in his prone attacker. When the paranormal groaned, Stanley didn't even think about it, knowing if the gargoyle got up again, he would just come after him again.

Stanley positioned the end of his gun's barrel at the gargoyle's temple and fired, and the rogue gargoyle collapsed onto his bed once more.

Swallowing around the bile that threatened to rise in his throat, Stanley backed away even as he reloaded. He pivoted, keeping half his attention on the downed gargoyle and peering into the front room. Stanley knew the remorse would come, having to take a life, even in self-defense, but that would be for later.

Right then, Stanley needed to figure out just what the fuck was going on.

Stanley took in the destruction of his cabin, the place that had been his sanctuary for over a decade. A large window had been shattered, strewing glass shards across half the floor. Tables and chairs had been crushed, his coffee table had been flattened, and the sofa and chairs were shredded. Five gargoyles had collapsed throughout the room, appearing to be in varying stages of healing.

Recognizing the closest gargoyle as Lebone, Stanley hurried to his side. He noticed the deep red slashes along his side and the tear in the male's wing. Grimacing, Stanley carefully lowered to one knee, using the butt of his rifle to steady himself.

Reaching down, Stanley searched for a pulse. To his relief, he found it. While it was sluggish, it was there. Stanley hoped that meant he was already healing and there wasn't some wound on his front causing him to bleed out. Unfortunately, Stanley knew he didn't have the strength to check.

Stanley spotted the earpiece in Lebone's ear and began reaching for it. Just as he touched it, he heard a roar, and his front door crashed open. Stanley stayed on his knees but snapped his rifle back to his shoulder, aiming it at the hulking, winged shadow in the doorway.

A second later, seeing Kultrak step forward, Stanley lowered his weapon. "Kultrak," he whispered. The adrenaline began seeping from his body, and he settled back on his calves. "What the hell happened?"

"Stanley," Kultrak cried, rushing to his side, seemingly oblivious to the downed gargoyles. He slid to his knees before Stanley and immediately gripped his upper arms. "Are you okay?" His expression appeared pained as Kultrak focused on his side. "You're bleeding again."

Stanley glanced down and spotted the fresh blood seeping into the bandage on his side. The resurgence of pain registered, too, as did something else. He'd been fighting naked.

Huh.

"I must have pulled a couple of stitches," Stanley stated. Patting Kultrak's chest, he tried to reassure him. "I'll be fine. Really."

"But you're bleeding again," Kultrak growled, shaking his head. "I was supposed to protect you."

Lifting his twenty-two so he could tap the butt of his rifle on the floor once, Stanley stated, "Kultrak, I'm not some fainting violet who can't defend himself. I can handle myself."

Grimacing, Kultrak hung his head even as he peered at him through his lashes. "But you were already injured," he whispered, sounding so damn upset.

"Yes, and now we have a lot of other injured," Stanley pointed out. Sliding his palm up Kultrak's chest, he noticed the slick blood coating his gargoyle's skin, wondering where it came from. "Including you." Once Stanley cradled Kultrak's jaw, Stanley used his hold to encourage his gargoyle to look toward the room. "Including them. We need to help our friends."

Stanley figured he could get answers once he managed to get Kultrak to focus on what was important—their downed friends.

Finally, Kultrak appeared to really take in the room's destruction. "Shit," he whispered.

"Yeah," Stanley muttered.

That about summed it up.

"Here." Kultrak grabbed a throw blanket from the floor that had once been on the back of the sofa. Then he began wrapping it around Stanley's body toga-style.

"Uh, right." Stanley accepted the impromptu wrap, wondering how he kept forgetting about his nudity.

Must be the adrenaline or pain.

Before more could be said, a pale-yellow gargoyle off to the right began to stir. Stanley didn't recognize him.

Kultrak leaped to his feet and stalked toward the downed gargoyle. Without a word, he reached down and slashed his claws over the male. In the next instant, the yellow gargoyle's head tipped away from his body, blood spraying across the floor.

Stanley grimaced, shaking his head. "Was that necessary?"

"He was a rogue, Stanley," Kultrak told him, staring at the downed gargoyle with a curled lip. "He didn't deserve to live, and our kind can come back from a helluva lot."

"But did you have to do it on my floor?" Stanley shook his head. "This mess was huge as it was."

"Sorry." Kultrak grimaced, taking in the mess he'd made. Peering at Stanley with contrition in his eyes, he told him, "I'll clean it up."

Nodding, Stanley peered around his home again. He wondered if there was anything salvageable. Then he realized it really wasn't the time for such worries.

"Just how much can a gargoyle come back from?" Stanley asked curiously.

"A lot," Kultrak repeated.

"A headshot?" Stanley glanced toward his bedroom.

Kultrak hesitated, then admitted, "Depending on the headshot. Yeah."

Wondering if he'd actually killed the gargoyle after all, Stanley pointed. "Then you may want to check the gargoyle on my bed."

"Your bed?" Kultrak snarled incredulously.

Stanley just shrugged, fatigue flooding him since the adrenaline was wearing off.

Rushing into the bedroom, Kultrak disappeared. A second later, he reappeared with a body wrapped in Stanley's comforter. Kultrak offered him a pained smile.

"I'll dispose of him outside, just in case."

Nodding slowly, Stanley reached down and rechecked Lebone's pulse, pleased to find that it had grown stronger. He used the butt of his rifle to push to his feet. Carefully, he moved across the room, avoiding shards of wood and broken glass as he headed to Lludd's side.

The pale purple gargoyle began to stir even before he reached him, so Stanley bypassed him to head to Biscane. The huge gargoyle lay sprawled on his back, eyes staring blankly at the ceiling. For just an instant, Stanley felt a clench in his gut as he feared the worst.

Then Biscane blinked before turning his head to peer at Stanley. His smile appeared a little wan. "Hey, man. Glad to see you all right." Biscane frowned as he focused on Stanley's midsection. "Mostly, anyway."

Biscane forced himself to a sitting position just as Kultrak returned. Nodding once at Biscane, he headed toward the final gargoyle that Stanley didn't recognize—a coral-colored beast with red wings and claws. To Stanley's surprise, Kultrak knelt beside him and checked for a pulse.

"He's alive," Kultrak stated, sounding relieved.

Stanley jumped to the only conclusion that made sense. "Not a rogue?"

Kultrak shook his head even as he watched Lludd rise unsteadily to his feet. "One of Elder Cliatno's men, who is not a threat, thankfully." Blowing out a breath, Kultrak started toward Stanley and Biscane. "A whole helluva lot of rogues were chasing him and his enforcers here," he explained, wrapping one arm around Stanley's waist to steady him while offering his other to Biscane to help him to his feet. "Hence all the fighting." Still looking annoyed, Kultrak grumbled, "I hate that you ended up involved, my mate."

"Your mate?" A lean black gargoyle staggered from the bathroom. His expression dripped with hatred and disdain as he took in the room. "You're mated with a *human*?" With a cold bark of laughter, the gargoyle turned toward the back door. "Elder Laagstine will love this information." Then the male ran out the back.

Stanley could see just well enough to watch him spread his wings and disappear into the sky.

Tensing beside him, Kultrak took one step before he froze.

Guessing at Kultrak's dilemma, Stanley encouraged, "You can go after him. I'll be fine here."

Kultrak still looked conflicted. Then he dipped his head and pecked a kiss to his temple before taking off. A second later, Kultrak disappeared out the door.

With a sigh, Stanley pressed a hand to his side.

"Stanley?" Biscane questioned.

"I'm okay," Stanley assured. "Really. Just popped a few stitches. It's good." Then he waved his hand, admitting, "This though. I don't even know where to begin."

"You don't need to begin tonight," Lludd told him, slipping over to Lebone's side. "And you won't have to do it alone, either."

"I checked Lebone's pulse earlier," Stanley told Lludd as he lowered to a knee beside the still-downed gargoyle. "His pulse was getting stronger."

Lludd nodded, then rolled Lebone to his back. The move revealed more gashes as well as where blood had pooled from a wound on his temple. With the way Lebone's left leg flopped oddly, making Stanley's stomach clench uncomfortably, it wasn't a surprise when Lebone moaned loudly.

"Damn," Lludd grumbled, rubbing the back of his neck. "That looks like it hurts."

"How's it looking in here?"

Stanley focused on the front door, spotting Gurrando there. Struano stood at his shoulder, obviously keeping watch over the elder. Both men hadn't gotten out of the fight unscathed, and there were various spots of blood with a few scratches mixed in.

"We'll need someone to set Lebone's leg, but we'll all live," Lludd stated, sliding his arms under the other gargoyle's prone body. He grunted as he rose, and even swayed a little once standing, but he managed to get his balance. "I'll take him to the bunkhouse."

"Bunkhouse?" Gurrando questioned, even as his attention fell on Stanley.

Stanley nodded. "When we ended up with so many mated gargoyles, Nicholas and Bodb added a wing to the bunkhouse," he explained, appreciating Biscane's assistance in moving toward the other gargoyle. "He created a couple of medical rooms, but we don't really have a medic. Just a couple of guys who had a bit of field medicine experience."

"We're definitely going to have to change that," Gurrando declared, stepping backward to allow them all to pass.

Stanley completely agreed. Noticing the way that Struano continued to watch the skies, he wondered if the danger had passed.

And where is Kultrak?

CHAPTER TEN

Kultrak was surprised at how swiftly the rogue gargoyle could fly, especially considering he'd appeared to have been injured at Stanley's house. Winging swiftly through trees, he barely managed to keep the other male in sight. Thinking he spotted a clearing ahead, he put on a burst of speed, hoping to drive him down into it.

When Kultrak was fifty yards from the tree line, a large body slammed into him, driving him sideways. He immediately went on the defensive, slashing in an attempt to pull free of the other gargoyle's grip. To Kultrak's surprise, the gargoyle didn't resist, and he immediately released him.

Spinning in midair, Kultrak faced his attacker, ready and willing to take out another rogue. To his surprise, he found himself staring at Ssimeas. Opening his mouth, he prepared to question Bodb's enforcer.

Ssimeas lifted one hand in placation as he flew before him. He placed his other finger before his lips, urging him to be silent.

While Kultrak still felt wary, he snapped his mouth shut and nodded once.

Crooking his fingers, Ssimeas began moving toward the clearing. He flew slowly and sank lower toward the ground. Ssimeas weaved between trees, keeping his wingbeats as silent as possible.

Kultrak decided to give the other enforcer the benefit of the doubt and did the same. Carefully, he followed the dark-blue male. As he drew closer, he realized he could hear voices.

Ssimeas perched on a tree branch. After he beckoned again, he began creeping along branches.

Doing his best to follow Ssimeas exactly, Kultrak followed. He glanced around warily, worried he was walking into a trap. Kultrak hadn't spent much time with any of Bodb's men, but Gurrando had always made it sound like they were above reproach.

"Yes, Chieftain. I saw it with my own eyes and heard the enforcer call him mate." Kultrak recognized the tenor-voiced speaker as the black gargoyle who'd been at Stanley's. "There were so many more paranormals here than what was reported. Dozens. That's why we failed. We need more men."

A low growly voice snarled, "I don't want to hear your excuses." That was followed by the unmistakable sound of someone backhanding another.

"Sorry, Chieftain," the black gargoyle murmured submissively.

"So," the second male—the chieftain—Kultrak wondered of what clutch—took on a snarling tone. "More gargoyles taking humans and other weaker paranormals as mates. No wonder they have to have so many together to think they're safe."

Evidently, the chieftain was buying the black gargoyle's story.

Finally, Ssimeas stopped. Reaching forward, he rested his palm on the branch in front of him. Carefully, he pushed down on the branch, revealing the clearing Kultrak had spotted in the distance.

Kultrak settled on the branch next to Ssimeas, digging his toe claws into the branch for balance. He frowned at what he saw. There were four gargoyles standing on the far side of the clearing. Three were big and broad, while the fourth was the leaner black male.

Looking them over, Kultrak felt his jaw sag open. *Not possible.* He recognized one of them . . . and he was supposed to be dead.

Ex-Chieftain Grecian.

Glancing toward Ssimeas, wondering if he recognized the male, too, Kultrak wasn't certain. He read the anger on the other gargoyle's face, but that was about it. Ssimeas had his jaw clenched tight, and his eyes were narrowed.

At least he's not in league with these rogues.

Kultrak had never been more relieved that one of his stray thoughts was proven incorrect. When Grecian began talking again, Kultrak refocused on the group.

"Let's get out of here," Grecian ordered, sweeping his gaze over the surrounding trees. "We need to report to Elder Laagstine. He'll need to know that those human sympathizers are gathering up the other elders." As Grecian started into the trees, his next comment floated on the wind back to Kultrak, making his blood run cold. "The elder will need to step up his plans to convert or wipe out the rest of the opposing elders before these traitors can get to them."

Tensing, Kultrak wanted nothing more than to go after the group. He felt certain that between himself and Ssimeas, they would be able to take them, even if it was two on four. Except, Ssimeas rested his hand on Kultrak's arm, drawing his attention.

When Kultrak focused on Ssimeas, the other gargoyle mouthed one word.

Mates.

Kultrak sighed deeply, nodding once. Ssimeas was right. They had a responsibility to think of the big picture.

If they were captured, not only could they be used against their elders, but it would put the lives of their mates in jeopardy. Kultrak never wanted that. The best action was to report back and gather intelligence.

Plus, they needed to warn their elders that the rest of the

Circle of Elders were in danger.

Turning on the branch, Kultrak followed Ssimeas back out of the trees. Once they were at a safe distance, they took to their wings. They stayed low enough to keep hidden amongst the treetops even as they sped as quickly as possible.

By the time they reached the ranch, quite a bit of guilt was plaguing Kultrak. Even with Stanley's blessing, he shouldn't have been so foolish as to go so far. Plus, he never should have considered plunging head-long into danger that way, attacking a group of rogues that he knew little about.

Kultrak wanted nothing more than to wrap his arms around his injured mate and to be certain that he was once again on the mend.

Gods, I hope he's on the mend.

That just made him feel even more guilty. He'd left his reinjured mate with another gargoyle. As he neared, he saw that clean-up was in full swing. A number of bodies had been stacked in a far clearing, and Kultrak figured they were disposing of the rogues via a funeral pyre.

It was the easiest way.

"You okay, Kultrak?" Ssimeas finally spoke, looking at him in concern. "I'm sure Stanley's fine. The guys won't let anything happen to any of our mates."

"I shouldn't have left him." Kultrak admitted his folly. "Fleeing rogue or not." Then he waved toward Ssimeas. "Besides, you were already tracking them."

Ssimeas smirked and shrugged. "You didn't know that. You were doing your job." After they landed near the back deck, Ssimeas patted him on the shoulder. "Stanley will understand that. He understands responsibility."

Kultrak heaved a sigh, letting go of some of his guilt. "Thank you," he stated heartfeltly, appreciating the other male's words. Peering around the area, Kultrak realized he didn't know where to go. He did feel certain that Stanley wouldn't still be in his cabin, but beyond that—"Uh, where?"

"Bunkhouse," Ssimeas told him, pointing. "That's where the injured would be taken." Indicating the main house, he told him, "I'm going to track down the elders and let them know we need to have a meeting." Ssimeas's brows furrowed as he shook his head, and his features hardened. "That big black gargoyle was Enforcer Whelan. What the hell was he doing with rogues?"

"That was Enforcer Whelan?" Kultrak asked, pausing where he'd already taken a couple of steps away from the other gargoyle. Kultrak had never met the enforcer who wasn't assigned a permanent elder. "You sure?"

Ssimeas nodded. "Yeah. Met him once when Elder Bodb needed an extra enforcer while traveling." Frowning, he muttered, "He was sort of a dick."

"A freelance enforcer gone rogue," Kultrak mused, shaking his head. "His years working at many other estates would definitely have given him the chance to gather plenty of intel on the elders."

Growling, Ssimeas curled his lip. "Hadn't thought of that."

"And now he's with ex-chieftain Grecian." Kultrak ran a hand through his hair in frustration. "Between them two and their comment about Laagstine, this isn't boding well."

"Grecian?" Ssimeas appeared shocked. "He was reported dead."

"Well, he's not." Kultrak cocked his head as he eyed Ssimeas. "One of our elders may want to find out who reported Grecian's termination."

Ssimeas scoffed. "You got that right." Then he turned and hustled into the house.

Turning toward the bunkhouse, Kultrak began jogging toward the building in search of his own mate. He paused outside the door, hesitating. He'd never actually been in the building, so he didn't know if he should knock.

Kultrak decided to do a combination. He knocked twice before gripping the knob and turning it. Considering it wasn't locked, he didn't feel bad about heading inside without an invitation.

Recognizing nearly all the men lurking about the main front room, Kultrak nodded a greeting. He eyed Biscane, taking in the gargoyle's frame. The large black gargoyle had a bandage over his left pectoral, and he had his arms clasped around the waist of a brown-haired human. It took Kultrak a few seconds, but he soon placed the scent as Jory, Biscane's mate.

Huh. Didn't think he was supposed to be here tonight.

Kultrak was quickly able to make out Jory muttering, "As soon as I heard, of course I came." The human sounded annoyed. "Why the hell would you think I'd stay away?"

"Because we were essentially attacked," Biscane rumbled back. "It'd dangerous."

Jory frowned at Biscane. "And that's exactly why I dropped everything and got my ass out here." Looking at Biscane as if he had two heads, the human continued, "My deposition can wait. Making certain everything is good with you is far more important."

Even as Kultrak felt the corners of his lips twitch, he looked around the room again, searching for someone who might have some answers for him. There was a plethora of scents spread across the room. Other than opening every door in the place, Kultrak wasn't certain how to track his mate.

"Hey." Kultrak turned left and spotted a human beckoning him. The male was older with plenty of gray around his temples and sprinkled throughout his dark-brown hair. "Stanley is this way."

Finally, Kultrak placed the older human as Keith, an unmated ranch hand. The man had been part of the place for nigh on thirty-five years and was loyal to Nicholas to the bone. When Nicholas had bonded with Bodb, there had been no question about bringing him into the know.

"Thanks," Kultrak responded, following. "How is he?"

"Pissed that we're forcing him to lie down," Keith told him dryly. The older male shook his head a couple of times before pausing at a door and staring at him. "Word of advice, son. Just do whatever's necessary to soothe him and get him to rest. Otherwise —" Scoffing, Keith didn't bother to finish his sentence.

Kultrak could guess. Stanley would stop being a docile patient. Considering he'd managed to rise from what was essentially his sick bed and take out a gargoyle all by himself — and Kultrak wasn't even certain where Stanley kept the rifle — meant his mate probably wouldn't want to be kept out of the loop from then on.

My mate is a warrior. I need to remember to treat him as such.

"Thanks for the advice, Keith," Kultrak replied, pausing at the door. He focused on the older man, trying to figure out when the last time someone had called him son. Dismissing the thought, since he couldn't remember, Kultrak asked, "Was anyone badly injured . . . other than Lebone?"

Kultrak recalled the gargoyle had a broken leg.

"Elder Cliatno's enforcer, the one who they were helping fly, has a broken arm and a hell of a head wound," Keith told him, shaking his head. "He'll heal, so Doc Glover says."

"Doc Glover?" Kultrak didn't recognize that name, and his tension ratcheted up a notch.

"Yep." Keith scoffed, obviously reading him. "Relax. He was the other guy helping the elder bring the enforcer to us." Shaking his head, Keith muttered, "Guess he'd been at the estate reportin' some other problem, but I haven't heard what yet." With a shrug, the human added, "Sort of above my paygrade." Then Keith waved toward the waiting door. "Best get in there, son. Your man's waited long enough."

With a nod, Kultrak knew the ranch hand was right. He gripped the knob and turned it quietly. Poking his head in,

Kultrak checked to see if Stanley was awake.

Not only was Stanley awake, but he was sitting up in bed talking with Lludd. The large gargoyle sat beside the bed and seemed to be explaining everything that had been going on. Even though Kultrak felt a little guilty that he hadn't been the one to share everything, he felt grateful that he wouldn't have to worry about doing it.

"Hey, baby," Kultrak greeted, smiling when Stanley focused on him. "How are you feeling?" From the calm look on his mate's features and the way his human eyed him, Kultrak wasn't completely certain. At least he didn't scent any anger or frustration in the air. "Can I get you anything?" Then he glanced toward Lludd and told the other gargoyle, "Thank you for sitting with him."

Lludd rose to his feet and rolled his wide shoulders in a shrug. "Didn't mind explaining what's been going on." As he walked past Kultrak, his rumbling voice contained a bit of a laugh as he said, "When I realized Arthur was my mate, I was encouraged to learn to communicate." Patting Kultrak on the shoulder as he passed him, Lludd advised, "You may want to try it."

"Right. Thanks," Kultrak muttered as Lludd made his way out. Then he refocused on Stanley, who he realized hadn't answered any of his questions. Crossing to the bed slowly, Kultrak again assessed his mate. "Uh, Stanley? You okay?"

To Kultrak's relief, Stanley patted the bed beside him.

Kultrak quickly settled beside him, cocking his knee up so he could half-face him. Focusing his sole attention on Stanley's face, he took his mate's hand between both of his own. His human didn't seem upset, but he definitely appeared serious as Stanley met his gaze.

"Did you catch that gargoyle?" Stanley asked softly.

Wincing, Kultrak shook his head. "That asshole was damn

fast. I tracked him to a clearing where he met a few other gargoyles." He didn't want to get into specifics, but he admitted,
"Ssimeas was there, too, and between us both, we recognized
two of the three he joined up with." With a shake of his head,
Kultrak admitted, "They're not good gargoyles."

Stanley nodded slowly, seeming to take that in stride.
"Well, I'm glad you're safe," he murmured. Then his black
brows drew together as he roved his gaze over Kultrak's
body. "You *are* okay, right?"

Pleased that Stanley expressed concern for him, Kultrak
smiled and nodded. "Just a few scratches while taking out a
gargoyle after Elder Cliatno while he was busy helping an enforcer make it to us," he explained. "It's why I couldn't get to
you sooner when I heard that several rogue gargoyles had
managed to corner Lebone and slam him into your roof."
Frustration caused Kultrak to shake his head as he held Stanley's gaze and said, "I am sorry about that, my mate." After a
second, he allowed his gaze to fall to the fresh bandages on
Stanley's side, and he asked, "A-Are you okay?"

"I'm fine," Stanley assured, squeezing his fingers. His dark
eyes grew intense as he peered at him. "And on that note, I
want you to bond with me." As Kultrak gaped at Stanley, having in no way expected that demand, Stanley continued, "I
won't be out of the loop again, and I need to be well to help
our family stay safe . . . and you."

Kultrak felt a swell of pleasure upon hearing Stanley's
words. While it wasn't a declaration of love, he knew they
would get there someday. Kultrak smiled and nodded.

"Anything you wish, my mate."

CHAPTER ELEVEN

Stanley opened his mouth, then snapped it closed again. Surprise filled him upon hearing Kultrak's immediate acceptance. He'd been mentally preparing a whole big spiel about why they should bond, even with him still injured. Kultrak's response had thrown him for a loop.

Clearing his throat, Stanley jerked a nod. "Okay then." He struggled with what to say next and decided on, "Then you better go lock the door."

"N-Now?" Kultrak still looked taken aback, even though he'd just agreed. "Like, *right now?* With everyone . . ." His focus strayed to the door and what was probably a pretty full bunkhouse.

Oh, how cute. My gargoyle is shy.

Smirking, Stanley reached over and slid open the nightstand closest to him. He dipped his hand inside, all the while holding Kultrak's gaze. When Stanley pulled out his hand, he waggled the tube of lube he'd drawn out.

"Yep."

Then Stanley waited, anticipation and worry mixing within him in equal measure.

After a few heart-stopping seconds, Kultrak's eyes narrowed, and he began stalking toward the door. "Now," he growled softly before turning back around to pin a feral gaze upon Stanley. "Under one condition."

A shudder of need worked down Stanley's spine upon hearing that delicious tone. "What's that?"

Stanley did his best to make his words come out strong, but

he knew he'd failed miserably. His cock had hardened nearly to the point of pain, and his body hummed with need. He damn near shivered with hot desire.

"You stay still and let me take care of everything," Kultrak declared, clicking the lock on the door. When Stanley opened his mouth to counter—he didn't know how he could manage that—Kultrak began stalking toward the bed, his features harsh, and told him, "I won't allow you to be hurt in any way." His voice lowered. "You're everything to me."

Stanley felt his emotions softening, and he smiled. "All I can do is promise to do my best," he told him. With a shrug, he added, "I'm not perfect, after all."

Kultrak plucked the tube of lube from Stanley's fingers, saying, "No one is perfect." Skimming the backs of his fingers along Stanley's side, causing a myriad of tingles to erupt on his flesh, Kultrak told him, "And I'd hate to think you are, since I'm certainly not."

Relaxing under Kultrak's soft touches, Stanley hummed as heat flooded every inch of him that the gargoyle touched. "Good," he mumbled. Pushing with his arms, he scooted down the comforter a little until he lay prone on the bed. "Now, pull off my sweats and fuck me, my gargoyle." Stanley loved the way a shudder appeared to work through Kultrak's big body when he heard the honorific. With a smile, he lifted a hand and beckoned. "Make me yours."

"You're already mine, Stanley," Kultrak declared roughly, tossing the lube onto the mattress. "This"—he cast a feral gaze over Stanley's partially-clad form, making him heat from the inside out and his cock jerk behind his sweatpants—"is just a formality."

Then Kultrak reached for the waistband of Stanley's sweatpants. Feeling the gargoyle's claws slide across the sensitive—and vulnerable—skin of his abdominals, then his groin as he pulled them down, caused a thrill to rush through Stanley.

His body flushed hot, and his erection twitched as the evening air of the bedroom ghosted over it.

"Gorgeous," Kultrak rumbled, drawing his sweats down and off Stanley's legs. "My amazing mate."

Kultrak's gaze filled with heat as he roved it over Stanley's frame, making him feel damn near ten feet tall. When the gargoyle skimmed his claws up his calves, then thighs, to rest in the grooves of his groin, Stanley nearly vibrated out of his skin. His erection ached in the best of ways, throbbing and leaking, begging for attention.

Stanley almost gave in to the urge to grab himself, needing release so very badly, until Kultrak picked up the lube.

A second later, Kultrak peered at him with an intense expression on his face. "This isn't the way I thought I would end up claiming my mate, Stanley," he told him gruffly. "But I'll never regret the gift you're giving me." Kultrak curled his tail around his body and poured a large dollop of lube on the tip even as he whipped his loincloth from his hips. "Don't ever forget that." As Kultrak climbed onto the bed and straddled Stanley, he rested one forearm on the mattress as he placed the now-closed lube on the pillow beside them. "I'll do my best to fulfill every one of your fantasies." Pausing, Kultrak sucked in a deep breath, his expression turning feral. "As soon as you're healed." Lowering his head, the gargoyle whispered right before he claimed Stanley's lips, "I can't wait to explore everything with you."

Then Kultrak's lips were on Stanley's, stealing his breath away as well as his thoughts. He gripped the gargoyle's thick upper arms, even as he did his best to keep his lower body still. Except for his legs, those he spread, anticipating that Kultrak would use his tail to open him.

He'd heard stories.

Except, after several minutes of Kultrak mapping his mouth, that didn't happen. His gargoyle broke the kiss on a groan, leaving Stanley panting harshly. He peered up at Kultrak's pale gray features, and he swore the male appeared to be flushed.

Stanley was about to question Kultrak — once he managed to draw enough breath — when he felt something unexpected. Groaning with pleasure, he barely resisted planting his feet and bucking up into the delicious squeeze on his cock. He snapped his eyes open and looked down, seeing a gray tail around his erection, jacking it and covering it with lube.

That was when Stanley remembered. A gargoyle bonded by both giving and receiving.

"Kultrak," Stanley cried, shock flooding him.

"Just relax and feel, my mate," Kultrak crooned as he levered up a little. His wings spread, offering him leverage as he positioned himself over Stanley's cock, using his tail to guide Stanley's erection to his entrance. "No strain on your stitches, remember?" Kultrak's face turned a little worried as he looked down at him, even as his chest heaved with his need. "Or we stop."

Stanley snarled. "No stopping," he declared, sliding one hand around Kultrak's shoulders. Hoping the rumors were true, Stanley wrapped his hand around the gargoyle's wing-joint where it connected with his shoulder blade while tugging the male downward. "Now."

Kultrak barked a cry and arched, pushing into Stanley's touch. The move caused his ass to sink closer to Stanley's groin. With his erection already poised at Kultrak's opening, his crown easily slipped inside the male. Stanley gasped and moaned as the delicious heat wrapped around his length, causing him to still as tingles of pleasure erupted within his groin.

"Naughty mate," Kultrak growled softly, gently easing Stanley's hand from his wing-joint. His expression feral, he held Stanley's gaze as he rocked on his erection, taking him deeper and deeper. "Just relax, Stanley," he crooned, rubbing up and down his torso as he slid him deeper. "Don't want you hurting yourself."

Stanley groaned even as his body shuddered. With his erection encased in the sweetest, most intense pressure he'd ever experienced, he couldn't even hope to find his tongue. He'd never taken anyone bare, and nothing could have prepared him for the exquisite bliss that Kultrak was offering him.

Instead, Stanley moaned and focused on doing as Kultrak ordered. After all, he knew the gargoyle was right. He breathed deeply and stilled his body — never had anything been so difficult in his life. Stanley wanted to buck up and rut so damn badly.

"Please," Stanley hissed, not above begging. Peering up into Kultrak's storm-cloud-colored eyes, he urged, "Please, I need you to move."

Kultrak growled and levered up a bit. "Gods, you feel good," he rumbled, resting his ass on Stanley's groin. His tail came forward again. "I'm going to ride you while I open you up, Stanley," he declared, grabbing the lube again. "Then I'm going to take you. We'll exchange bites and blood or both, and we'll be bonded for eternity."

As Kultrak spoke, he poured more lubricant onto his tail. Before Stanley could formulate a thought in his head other than, "Move," his gargoyle rested his hands on either side of his shoulders. Then . . . he did exactly that.

Stanley gasped as Kultrak slid up, halfway off his cock, before sinking back onto him. Doing it again, the gargoyle squeezed his rectum muscles, massaging Stanley's prick, creating a riot of delicious tingles. Kultrak did it again and again and again . . . then he began to trill.

Opening his mouth on a silent cry, Stanley jolted. His groin erupted with fiery tendrils that spread through every inch of his body. He trembled as tingles worked down his spine, settling in his ball sack.

A second later, it was too much. Stanley's orgasm slammed into him, sending his senses soaring. He shuddered and trembled as he spurted his cum deep within the gargoyle's body. Bliss sang through Stanley's veins as Kultrak's trilling extended his pleasure beyond anything he'd ever experienced.

When Stanley slowly came back to himself, he hummed with pleasure. His body still felt primed and ready even while being mixed with sated endorphins. He shivered and moaned, realizing Kultrak was easing off his shockingly still-hard prick.

"Mmmm, there you are, my mate," Kultrak rumbled, lowering to buss a kiss to his lips. Nuzzling Stanley's temple with his own, he murmured huskily, "Now I take you. We share blood and finish the bond."

Stanley hummed, liking the sound of that.

When Kultrak eased a bit away from him, Stanley had to blink a few times to focus on the gargoyle's face. He furrowed his brows, not liking the concern on his lover's features. It completely belied the thick rod Stanley could feel sliding against his thigh.

"What's wrong, my gargoyle?" Stanley asked softly. Using one hand, he cradled Kultrak's square jaw. "I won't deny you."

"I just hate the idea of hurting you."

Seeing the warmth within the depths of Kultrak's gray eyes, Stanley smiled. "I feel your tail in my ass," he teased, finally registering what was causing that extra sensation coursing through his body. "I hardly think you're going to hurt me."

Unfortunately, that didn't seem to ease Kultrak's concern. Fortunately, he admitted, "I can't think of too many positions that won't cause pressure on your torso." He appeared so upset by that. "I don't want to hurt you to complete our bond."

Sighing, Stanley revealed, "I've thought of one."

Kultrak appeared to relax. "Yeah?"

Nodding, Stanley murmured, "It's not exceptionally romantic, but it'll do the trick." With a wink, he added, "We'll do romantic another time."

"Definitely," Kultrak confirmed with a sly grin, making Stanley wonder what the gargoyle was thinking. Instead of telling him, he asked, "What do you suggest?"

"Position me on the side of the bed, my ass on the end, with my feet on those two footstools." Stanley indicated the stools that were in front of a pair of chairs that made up the small suites' living space. "Then kneel between my thighs, and well—" Unable to fight his blush, Stanley muttered, "Well, you get the idea."

Kultrak growled softly even as he nodded. "Got it." After a quick hard kiss to Stanley's lips, he held his gaze and told him, "We'll definitely do romantic another time."

Then Kultrak eased away, taking his tail with him—*too bad*—and moved the furniture in place. He carefully positioned Stanley's body, then guided his prick to Stanley's lubed and stretched hole. Kultrak held his gaze as he skimmed the backs of his forefingers down his cheek.

"My brave warrior mate," Kultrak murmured.

Before Stanley could respond, Kultrak pushed.

With a surprised hiss, Stanley felt his gargoyle's massive intrusion. He breathed slow and deep, accepting his lover's long, thick rod. Stanley felt stretched beyond anything he'd ever before experienced . . . and it didn't make his cock wane one little bit.

When Kultrak began rocking his hips, pegging his gland over and over, Stanley moaned his gargoyle's name. It took every bit of self-control to keep from wrapping his legs around the male's waist and rocking into his deep, sensual ruts. Only the fact that his torso already twinged kept him from doing it.

Fortunately, Stanley didn't have to control himself long. The way Kultrak pegged his prostate over and over with un-erring accuracy sent him soaring faster than he could ever have thought possible. Heat bloomed through his system.

Within moments, another orgasm roared through Stanley's body, and he shuddered and twitched beneath his growling gargoyle's rutting form, the male extending his bliss with each thrust.

Kultrak's bite nearly caused his eyes to roll to the back of his head, and Stanley vaguely wondered what that would feel like when he wasn't already spaced from pleasure.

When Kultrak offered Stanley his blood from his wrist, he happily accepted it, surprised to find the iron-rich fluid ex-tremely pleasing.

As Stanley succumbed to sleep, relaxing in Kultrak's strong arms, he wondered what would happen if he bit the gargoyle back.

CHAPTER TWELVE

With his arm wrapped firmly around Stanley's waist, Kultrak kept his mate's back securely pressed against his chest. He listened as the trackers reported in. It seemed there were gargoyles still out there watching them.

That didn't surprise Kultrak.

If I knew where the assholes were holed up, I'd surely keep an eye on them, too.

Kultrak didn't like that they still hadn't figured out where soon-to-be ex-elder Laagstine and his associates were hiding.

Over the past week, Gurrando and Bodb's people had managed to extricate two more elders — Proatai and Rhodes. For safety's sake, Elder Korsair had also decided to join them. Plus, they'd confirmed that Elder Vermidian in Wyoming was well protected within his vampire mate's coven.

That meant there were five more elders they needed to touch base with and secure the safety of . . . not counting figuring out what happened to Elder Rayzon.

I damn sure hope he wasn't killed.

Kultrak had always considered Rayzon a good male, but he didn't hold out much hope of finding him alive. If he was still living, Kultrak couldn't even guess what kind of torture he must have been enduring.

"Wait, what did you say, Sindrid?"

Stanley spoke up, refocusing Kultrak's attention on the group. They were supposed to be sharing any instances where they'd noticed scents of outsiders. They were trying to put together locations of possible encampments.

"Uh, which part?" The brown gargoyle furrowed his black eyebrow ridges. "That I discovered an unfamiliar scent while reviewing the north boundary or that I'd spotted a downed fence east of Willow Meadow?"

Kultrak figured it was a fair question. With Stanley being the ranch foreman, maybe he was worried about the cattle. After all, while he was still healing and hadn't been able to check fences himself — accelerated healing could only do so much considering they'd completed their bond only a week before — perhaps he was concerned about the cattle.

Stanley narrowed his eyes. "The part about tracking the unfamiliar scent north to the river."

Sindrid nodded. "Yeah. I lost him at that chasm. The one with the river that's fifteen feet down." Grimacing, he rubbed the back of his neck. "I figure he swooped down there, but I couldn't tell if he went upstream or down."

Nodding, Stanley murmured, "Yeah, the air currents would have disrupted anything pretty quickly except the smell of water."

"How do you —" Sindrid began, but Stanley seemed to be ignoring him.

"Hey, Gladstone," Stanley cut in, turning his attention to Bodb's middle brother. "Didn't you say something about scenting intruders below Wildflower Falls?"

Gladstone nodded. "I did."

The gargoyle had given his report prior to Sindrid.

Stanley snapped his fingers before glancing around at the group. "I think I know where they may be hiding."

Bodb cocked his head while Nicholas took a step forward. "Where?" both men asked right before Bodb yanked Nicholas back to his chest.

Yep. I'm not the only one feeling overprotective, considering the threat we're facing.

Clearing his throat, Stanley suddenly scented of unease.

Confused, Kultrak dipped his head and nuzzled his neck.

"What is it, my mate?" He knew that Stanley was loyal to the bone, so he couldn't fathom what could cause his reaction.

Stanley tipped his head to the side a little, offering Kultrak more room. "Uh, midway up the falls, there's a ledge. It's difficult to get to," he explained.

Kultrak noticed his mate didn't answer his question, but he didn't press the issue. *I'll ask again when we're alone.* Instead, he reveled in how the human seemed to draw strength from his touch.

"It leads to a secluded clearing hidden on the other side of the falls," Stanley told everyone. "I think their scouts are probably hiding there. You'd never scent them due to the water currents, and you'd never spot them from above or below due to the natural camouflage."

"How do you know about the place?" Nicholas asked, clearly curious.

Giving a half-shrug, Stanley told him, "I've ridden damn near every inch of this ranch." He chuckled depreciatively before adding, "Plus, my father took me there when I was young. He told me stories about how our ancestors would gather there before a hunt and offer prayers to the spirits." After a second, Stanley admitted, "And I like to go there a few times a year to meditate."

"Those times we thought you were going into the city for a night or two," Nicholas mused, a warm smile curving his lips. "You were there instead."

"A few times," Stanley admitted.

"Okay," Bodb cut in, getting them back on track. "Can you give us directions on how to get there? Is there a way to get a drop on those in the clearing?"

Stanley shook his head, making Bodb frown. "I don't think I can adequately describe the way." His human rubbed at the back of his neck, teasing around the gorgeous claiming bite Kultrak had left on his neck. Kultrak wondered if his mate was aware that he did it, perhaps drawing strength or reassurance from it. Stanley glanced up at Kultrak with a worried expression before meeting Bodb's gaze and saying, "I'll need to take whoever you want to send."

"No way," Kultrak instantly snarled.

There was no way Kultrak wanted Stanley anywhere near the rogues again.

Stanley's worried expression morphed into a frown. "Kultrak, we need to catch and get rid of the guys watching us." When Kultrak just continued to frown at Stanley, his mate sighed and told him, "I have no desire to fight another gargoyle, but these guys may have valuable information. What if they know where Elder Rayzon is?" Wincing, Stanley finished softly, "Or his body, at least."

Kultrak sighed, knowing Stanley was right, no matter how much he didn't like it. Nodding, he growled softly before declaring, "Very well. But I'm taking you." Giving his mate a hard look, he ordered, "And you don't leave my side. Got it?"

Nodding, Stanley smiled. "Agreed."

"Okay, how long does it take to get there?" Bodb asked. "If we can get there during the daylight, we'll have the advantage."

"How do you figure?" Nicholas asked.

The answer clicked in Kultrak's mind, and he answered, "Because all those instances of catching the whiff of intruders happened at night." He glanced around at the nearly a dozen gargoyles filling the room. "Didn't it?"

It hadn't been specified, but Kultrak would definitely bet on it.

The gargoyles who'd been giving reports began to nod, almost as one.

"Then we take reinforced nets and manacles," Bodb declared, a feral smile curving his lips. "Catch them while they're roosting and bring them in for questioning before we put them down."

Nicholas grimaced as he stared at the floor, but he didn't counter his mate.

Kultrak felt Stanley tense in his arms, and he realized his mate felt the same unease. Still, his human didn't say anything, either. They might not like the fact that they would need to kill the rogues, but the men understood it. For the safety of paranormals and humans everywhere, those wanting to cause harm needed to be stopped.

"Well, I would normally put a few supplies into my truck and get close via access road B," Stanley told them, finally answering Bodb's earlier question. "Then I'd hike in. That would take me about . . . uh, forty minutes in the truck and an hour hike." After a few seconds of hesitation, Stanley stated, "I could get there in a little over two hours by horseback. It's pretty tough terrain out there."

"By flying, it shouldn't take nearly that amount of time," Kultrak declared, eager to get the task taken care of. Especially since that meant at least some of the danger to Stanley would be passed. Kultrak peered out the window at the sun shining through. "We still have a few hours before sunset."

Kultrak had never been a gargoyle to wonder about what everything looked like during the day. He'd accepted that he was a creature of the night. That didn't change the fact that he appreciated all the extra hours he could spend with his mate now that he'd bonded with him.

Stanley had also done a fantastic job of reassuring Kultrak that his human form — with his pale skin reminiscent of an albino, long white hair, and muscular body — pleased him just as much as his true form.

Now I have many more hours to love on my mate.

"Everyone, gear up," Bodb ordered, peering around the room, his expression feral. "Let's get these bastards in our territory."

With his arm securely around Stanley, Kultrak turned and

began following the others as they streamed out of the room. He'd been impressed with the tech room that Lludd had shown him two days prior. The elder's people were a mix of many species, sharing their experience and expertise, and they seemed to have found a way to get all the toys.

"Wait a minute," Nicholas grumbled as Kultrak moved through a doorway. He paused and looked over his shoulder, but it became apparent that the man was focused on Bodb and wasn't speaking to them. "You don't think you're going, too, do you?"

Bodb opened his mouth, appearing a little sheepish, before he replied, "Of course, I'd like to go."

Kultrak could see an argument brewing, so he hurried after the others, having no desire to see how the elder resolved such issues with his human.

Once Kultrak and Stanley had been fitted with earpieces, he declined the thigh holster and firearm. He figured he should learn how to use it, but since he didn't have any experience with them yet, it would be more dangerous if he tried. Instead, Kultrak accepted a couple of large knives.

"I have my own that I need to get," Stanley countered when offered his choice of weapons. After pecking a kiss to Kultrak's lips, Stanley told him, "I'll meet you on the deck in a few minutes."

As much as Kultrak didn't want Stanley out of his sight, he knew he couldn't keep him at his side all the time. His mate was a strong, vibrant human, and he needed to respect that. It was part of what he'd come to love about Stanley, and even as protective as Kultrak was, he refused to smother that.

I'll find a balance.

With that in mind, Kultrak returned his attention to Spieron and accepted the cable cuffs he handed to him. He admired the heavy design and hoped he never ended up in them. Turning them this way and that, he couldn't imagine a gargoyle being able to cut through the weaved metal.

Kultrak headed out to the deck and waited as the group assembled. He found that Nicholas must have won the argument because Bodb wasn't going. Instead, they were both staying behind with several others, including Gladstone, Lebone, Sindrid, and most of the other paranormals who couldn't fly, in order to guard those who were currently roosting. The exception was Claude and Darian, who would be flown by a couple of gargoyles and strategically placed on overwatch.

"Keep in touch, guys," Bodb ordered, his arm around Nicholas. "Stay safe."

The elder didn't seem upset at all with having to stay behind, and Kultrak absently wondered what Nicholas had promised the gargoyle to pacify him.

Then again, maybe I don't want to know.

As Stanley approached, Kultrak admired his human. Under his form-fitting shirt, his mate still had a bandage covering the stitches in his side. Doc Glover assured them that they would probably need to be removed in the next day or so. Stanley moved much more freely, hardly favoring his right side at all, and Kultrak appreciated seeing his human so much more comfortable.

The fact that Stanly was armed with a knife on his thigh and carried his rifle shouldn't have turned Kultrak on, but it did.

So fucking sexy.

Sweeping Stanley into his arms, Kultrak spread his wings. "I love having you in my arms," he rumbled, pressing a lingering kiss to his mate's lips, loving that his human returned the move eagerly.

A deep voice clearing his throat drew Kultrak's attention, and he ended the kiss and looked around. Spotting a number of amused looks, he focused on Ssimeas. He expected Bodb's high-ranking enforcer to be leading.

Ssimeas grinned. "When you're ready, Kultrak."

Kultrak winced, realizing everyone was waiting on him. "Uh, right." He glanced at his mate in his arms. "Stanley knows the way."

Ignoring the chuckles, Kultrak bent his knees, spread his wings, and leaped. He hadn't carried someone while flying in decades, but he quickly acclimated to his mate's weight. Following where Stanley indicated, he flew northward.

After fifteen minutes of flying, Stanley pointed at the river cutting through the trees. "Follow downriver," his mate ordered.

Kultrak complied. The river soon sank between two banks of rocks, deeper and deeper. The water had long since created a channel between the stone, and tall pines guarded it on either side. In the distance, Kultrak made out the unmistakable sound of a waterfall.

The misty spray of the falls appeared before the actual cascade of water. Pausing above it, Kultrak admired the sight. The river poured out of the chasm to fall nearly sixty feet into a large pool before continuing between the trees.

"I don't see a clearing," Ssimeas stated from where he hovered beside them.

Stanley pointed. "It's there," he claimed, sounding certain. He pointed to an area about halfway up. Indicating to the right, he stated, "We'll need to land there and take the trail up."

"Okay," Ssimeas replied simply. As he moved in that direction, he ordered Lludd, who was carrying Claude, "Set them up in the tops of those pines." The blue gargoyle smirked at the human. "If anyone flies away that you don't recognize, you know what to do."

The human sniper nodded once. "Done."

Ssimeas gave the man a feral smile before heading to where Stanley had instructed. They followed Kultrak's mate, and Stanley revealed a path that looked little more than a game trail. If Kultrak had been out there alone, he would have completely overlooked it.

Tucking his wings close, Kultrak kept close behind Stanley as he led the way up the side of the cliff. Just as he'd told them, halfway up, the trail reached a small ledge that led toward the falls. Stanley ducked behind the curtain of moving water, and Kultrak quickly followed.

Instead of a cave, as Kultrak had surmised, on the other side of the falls, a large meadow appeared. The light barely filtered into the space, towering pines casting long shadows over the area in sweeping rays. The place had an almost ethereal feeling to it, and Kultrak could understand why Stanley's ancestors would use it as a place to commune with the spirits.

Unfortunately, the clearing was also empty—no roosting gargoyles.

"Damn," Ssimeas muttered, shaking his head. "I'd really hoped Stanley was right."

Kultrak had hoped so, too.

Stanley smirked as he chuckled. "You just need to know where to look," he told them. Then he moved deeper into the clearing. "There are nooks all over where my ancestors left gifts to the spirits. I bet—" Stanley stopped next to a massive pine and pulled aside a large bow, revealing a bowl-like space . . . and the figure of a roosting gargoyle. "Bingo."

"Hot damn, Stanley." Ssimeas grinned broadly. "Okay, guys. Spread out and start searching."

"Be respectful of this place," Stanley cautioned.

"Absolutely," Ssimeas agreed before cautioning the others. "No damage if possible."

The others agreed and quickly began searching.

"Come on, my mate," Kultrak urged, wrapping his arm around Stanley. Dipping his head, he nuzzled Stanley's neck. "Time for us to go home."

Stanley nodded even as he grinned impishly at him. "I definitely like the sound of that," he told him, allowing Kultrak to lead him back to the waterfall. Once they reached the ledge, Stanley paused and grinned at Kultrak. "Just gotta take care of one more thing."

"What's that?" Kultrak asked, even as he admired the view. They were almost thirty-five feet up, and he could see for miles.

Before Kultrak realized what Stanley was doing, his mate pulled away from him. He heard his mate let out a loud, happy-sounding war whoop as he leaped. In shock and awe, Kultrak watched Stanley make a graceful swan-dive into the pool so far below.

"Oh, gods," Kultrak grumbled, shaking his head. "My mate is going to test whether or not a gargoyle can have a heart attack."

Seeing Stanley's head pop up in the middle of the water, a huge mischievous grin on his face, Kultrak leaped and followed the man who held the other half of his soul into the pool below.

ABOUT THE AUTHOR

Charlie started writing fantasy when she was eight, and after stumbling onto her first erotic romance at age nineteen, she realized her true calling. She now focuses on writing gay erotic romance, normally of the paranormal variety, with heroes of all kinds. With the help and support of her husband, Charlie finally fulfilled one of her life-long goals . . . move to acreage with her horses. You can often find her curled up with her laptop and a cup of tea or glass of wine, creating her next adventure. Charlie enjoys exploring the mountains of her new Oregon home on horseback, 4-wheeler, or motorcycle.

She can be reached at ch.richards2010@yahoo.com

Or visit her at www.charlie-richards.com.

www.ingramcontent.com/pod-product-compliance
Lightning Source LLC
Chambersburg PA
CBHW070457130626
46555CB00003B/1042